THE HUNTED

NAMELESS - BOOK THREE

NIKKI ROBB

THE HUNTED

NAMELESS - BOOK THREE

NIKKI ROBB

ISBN: Paperback: 978-1-964036-08-3
ISBN: Hardback: 978-1-964036-18-2

This novel is a work of fiction, any similarities to real people and events are entirely coincidental.

Cover Design by Nicole Tuttle
Interior Design by Rachel McEwan
Printed and distributed by Kindle Direct Publishing

First Printing Edition

CONTENT WARNINGS

This novel includes and alludes to things that may be concerning, such as murder, violence, vampires, blood drinking, graphic sex, sexual assault, mentions of past trauma with rape, loss of a loved one to cancer, descriptions of torture, death of a parent, and family member, victim-blaming, panic attacks, brief thoughts of self-harm, PTSD, discrimination, hate crimes, parental neglect, and harassment.

Please consider these before continuing.

To everyone who didn't want Elena to have to choose
between Damon and Stefan.

In this book, she gets to keep them both. And then
some.

ARCHER

PROLOGUE

Being a Hunter means protecting the night from the monsters operating in the dark, risking your life to save people, and doing anything necessary to bring those creatures down.

Even if it puts innocent people in danger.

Nisi Nox.

If given the choice between one human life and a hundred, the choice is obvious. Or at least, it should be.

It used to be.

No one warns you how much harder it is when the life at stake is someone you care about. Those superhero movies lie to you. They make it seem like you can save both the girl *and* the bus full of citizens. But that's a lie. You have to choose.

I had to choose.

In the heat of the moment, it felt right and impactful—what I was doing to these creatures. While they choked on the toxic mixture I subjected them to, struggling for breath and scrambling to escape, it felt like I'd done something right. I had protected innocent people. I made the night and the world a safer place.

Nisi Nox.

But when the adrenaline slipped away and the fog settled, suddenly, there were bodies at my feet and a lump in my throat. How do you know who's the hero and who's the villain? And what happens if you're neither?

Not good enough to be a hero and not bad enough to be a villain.

Just not enough.

I suppose the perspective you're meant to adopt is the one that's handed to you. The viewpoint you hear the most often usually becomes the one you identify with, doesn't it? The victors write history, and the hero is typically the protagonist.

But the same story told from both sides might change your mind. Or it might not, but at least you'd have all the information. Maybe Athena will understand once she hears my side. Maybe she won't. I am safe because I fought for my safety, and I fought for hers. I want to be the hero in her story, to protect her from the clutches of these creatures.

I just hope she hasn't already picked her side.

ATHENA

ONE

I don't know what death feels like, so I could be dead right now, and I wouldn't even know it. I've recently learned that being 'dead' doesn't necessarily mean that you're 'not alive,' so it's anyone's guess. My body certainly felt like it had gone through a ridiculous amount of trauma. There was a buzzing sound that continued its persistent, angry assault on my ears, growing stronger each moment that my consciousness came back to me.

Alive then, I decided. I don't know for sure, but I can't imagine I'd still be in this much pain had Lady Death come to sweep me away.

A faint smell permeated the air, no, not the air. It felt like the scent was attached to me, stuck on my skin. I wasn't able to break free from its acidic nature. Light began to seep through the darkness, through small cracks in my eyelids as they rose, heavy and labored. Blinking, I adjusted to the sight before me. I was in an office. A massive wooden desk sat steadfast in the center of the room, an oversized chair resting behind it, empty. Bookcases lined the walls. I could have been fooled into believing this was a regular office had it not been for the cases of weapons that taunted me. Sharpened knives, crossbows, guns and ammunition, and wooden stakes. Dozens of them. Pointed and stained with a dark red, nearly black, blood. The type of stain that told me this weapon had taken more than one life. I felt sick and leaned forward to pull my eyes from them.

My heart pounded in fear and worry. Where were my mates? Were they alive? Were they safe? Were they here?

That's when I felt my hands bound behind me. Rough rope dug into the flesh at my wrists. Panic began to crest as I pulled against my restraints. Cries escaped my mouth as I struggled, to no avail. I hated feeling so weak.

I couldn't even free my fingers to brush against the bond on my wrist. I couldn't focus on my mates because of the fear; it was too potent and overwhelming. My chest heaved as I felt the panic beginning to sink its claws into my heart.

Instantly, a thought took root in my mind.

If I was a vampire, I could have saved them. I could escape.

It was a shock as the thought crossed my mind. I mean, sure, I had considered that possibility. Whenever I thought about what a future could look like for me and my mates, there was only one way we all ended up happy, and that was if I was turned. I didn't really understand the process or the consequences, and I couldn't imagine being so hungry that I might rip into Davia's throat at the next movie night. So, I didn't say anything. I hadn't vocalized the truth that it was something I could have wanted. Something I still wanted.

But here in this dimly lit room, tied to a chair, afraid, in pain, and tired of being weak, the thought was clear, clarified in the crucible of our situation. If I was a vampire, I could have saved us. I could have saved myself. I could get out of here. I wouldn't be stuck. I wouldn't be trapped. I wouldn't be so goddamn weak.

My eyes scanned the room quickly. "Ok, Athena, four things you can see…" I struggled. "Weapons… desk, there's a…it's a chair, then there's a… window," I whispered. "Three things… Three things," I closed my eyes tight, holding them shut against the onslaught of fear that stole my breath. "Three things…" I gasped. My mind slipped to Archer. The friend I had gotten to know, the person who had protected me, cared for me and came to my rescue. How had I been so blind? How did I let my guard down again? How did I let myself trust the wrong person? Again.

Tears streamed down my face, and I thrashed against my restraints. "Help!" I screamed. Unable to contain the urge anymore.

My throat burned from whatever substance was used to knock me out. I didn't notice the door had opened until a blurred silhouette made its way into my tearful vision. I pushed back against the chair, trying to move away, but I could not get even an inch of distance between myself and the visitor.

"Please, please…" I cried out.

"Athena." The sound of his voice sent an icy jolt of warning down my spine. "I'm so sorry."

"Fuck you," I spat up at him. As my vision cleared, I took him in. His green eyes were tired, and his black-dyed hair looked shaggy and unkempt.

"I guess I deserve that," Archer responded, slowly moving further into the space. I cringed back.

"Stay away from me, you monster!" I screamed. His hands rose in front of him.

"Athena, please. I can explain everything, but you must listen to me."

I laughed, a wicked, exasperated sort of cackle. "Listen to you? You drugged me, you knocked me out, you tied me to a fucking chair!" A painful memory returned to me. "You had Silas in the back of your truck! Where the fuck are they?" I demanded.

"Do you know what they are?" He asked with an edge of anger. I felt an eerie chill pass through me as the thought solidified.

"Do you?" I seethed.

He sighed, running a hand down his face.

"I do," he answered, finally. Looking at Archer, I didn't see any trace of the music-loving, kind-hearted man I'd gotten to know. Here in front of me was a stranger. His strong arms were weapons, and his eyes were a trap. He wore dark jeans and a white t-shirt, but the weapon he so often had hidden in his waistband was on full display—a wooden stake.

Was that the only way to kill a vampire? There was so much I didn't know about my mates. So much time I lost because of my fear. There is so much I might never get the chance to learn.

I felt sick.

"Let them go," I begged with a quiet intensity.

"I can't do that." He took another step forward, but I snarled in his direction. "They are monsters, Athena. Vampires." He waited for my response. I didn't give him an inch.

"Maybe you haven't noticed, but you're the one who kidnapped five people," I growled at him. He winced, and I might have felt sorry if I cared about him.

"Not people, vampires," he corrected.

"Then what the fuck am I?" I screamed, and the air hung thick between us. "A casualty?" He stared me down, something resembling sadness in his gaze.

"I'm trying to keep you safe," he argued, a sort of pleading tone to his words. I scoffed at him.

"By tying me to a fucking chair and chloroforming me?"

He took a frustrated breath and threw his hands up. "I am a Hunter. I kill vampires, and I protect humans. It's what I do."

Kill.

That word sent a sharp pain through my chest. I would have fallen to my knees if I wasn't bound to the chair. They can't kill my mates. Oh my god. What if they had already? I wouldn't survive that.

"Where are they?" I asked in a whisper, afraid that anything louder would send me toppling into a spiral I wouldn't recover from.

"They're locked up," he responded, equally as quietly.

"Alive?"

It was his turn to scoff.

"They aren't alive, Athena. They're vampires."

I rolled my eyes.

"So what's your big plan here, Archer?" I spat his name as if it were a dirty word. "Kill them, and then finish me off because I've seen too much?"

He wore a shocked expression. "Of course not," he stammered. "I won't let them hurt you."

"You're the one hurting me!" I ushered back quickly.

"We can go back and forth on this all day," he groaned, running a hand through his hair. "The point is, I did what I did to protect you. I had hoped you'd be able to see that."

"Yeah well, I don't."

We stared at each other for a few silent moments. He started to turn.

"What are you going to do to me?" I asked, trying not to let my fear quiver in my voice.

He looked back at me over his shoulder, his green eyes gleaming with unshed tears. "I'm going to protect you. Even if that means protecting you from yourself." And then he was gone. And I was alone.

ORPHEUS

TWO

Vampires are some of the most indestructible creatures on this Earth. If not *the* most indestructible. Our skin can be pierced, but unless it's a wooden stake to the heart, it doesn't do any lasting damage. We can be shot, take literal bullets to our chest, arms, hell, even our throats, and still we'd heal. We'd have one hell of a scar, but at least we'd still be breathing. Our hearts would still beat once per hour. We can survive plane crashes, bombings, and diseases. We can live forever—century after century.

So why is it that our indestructible nature can be so easily thwarted by a mixture of aerosolized garlic and water that's been prayed over by a priest?

I should have known what they would try and that we weren't safe there. But I didn't, and now my coven was paying for that mistake.

Athena.

Fuck.

Just the thought of my stunning mate being left behind made me want to rip someone's throat out. As my vision blurred and my consciousness faded, it was her voice that I heard. Her scared cries, her anxious breathing. If they hurt her…

My eyes adjusted to the darkness of my cell. I could freak out, I could thrash against the bars, I could threaten death, I could do a lot of things. However, that tactic didn't work the first time, and I've spent a lot of energy these last few years preparing for this exact scenario. I knew that Nameless would catch up to us one day, and we would be right back here. The others focused their energy on staying out of their clutches while I'd been preparing for what to do when we returned. Some may consider that a pessimistic mindset, but I knew the reality of what was chasing us. I knew that if nobody was going to be realistic, I had to be.

Despite the plans, I couldn't help the anger that it had come to it. Just because you prepare for a storm doesn't mean you want to be caught in the eye of it.

As I pressed my face against the bars and peered out, the long, narrow hallway stretched before me like a serpent's den. The air was damp and heavy with the musty scent of decay, and a pervasive silence enveloped the corridor, broken only by the faint echoes of distant water droplets dripping onto the cold floor. The stone walls were rough and uneven, covered in patches of moss and grime, with the occasional flicker of faintly glowing fluorescent, providing the only source of feeble illumination. As I stood there, taking in the sight of the familiar and foreboding dungeon, the familiarity was like an ashen taste in my mouth. I shivered as my eyes scanned the scratches along the cell's back wall. Like a rabid animal was once held within these bars. I guess I was in a bit of a mindless frenzy when I made those marks. How thoughtful of the Hunters to place me back in my old cell. Unfortunately, in this case, familiarity does not breed content.

I came to rather quickly. It was faster than the Hunters expected but not fast enough to avoid being tossed in here. Having Athena's fresh blood in my system was like a jump start. Her potent blood would keep us strong for at least a week. Longer than they expect. We can use that. That will help my plan. We just have to be smart about it.

"Fuck!" I heard Silas exclaim from the cell to my left. A metallic clanging sound permeated the air, and his growls of effort echoed down the stone hallway.

"Silas," I called out, pressing against the bars. Still, he raged on. "Silas," I commanded again.

"We've gotta get out of here," he growled, anger, pain, fear. His emotions slammed into me like a freight train, and I held onto the bars to stave off the onslaught.

"I know. Please save your energy for when it will count." That seemed to appease him a little bit.

Just then, two more sets of emotions slammed into me.

"Samara, Laz, are you hurt?" I asked. I heard soft groans as they came to. It was a few moments before Laz responded.

"Nothing I can't handle." Their southern drawl was thicker than usual, as it tended to be when they were under pressure.

"Samara?" I called.

I felt her grief so potently. Being here isn't easy for any of us, but there's a certain special kind of torture reserved just for her.

"They put me in her cell." Her voice was timid, soft, and weak. None of the rest of us spoke. There weren't any words. There would never be words. "She…" Samara started, but sobs wracked her chest.

We listened to her fall apart in silence.

But we would not be silent forever. Nameless was going to regret ever crossing The Wanderers.

As Samara's grief floated about, dancing in my senses, I felt a shock of fear and anger so thick and volatile that I knew it could only belong to her—my mate.

"I feel her," I spoke aloud.

"Athena?" Laz clarified.

"Yeah, I can feel her." I let out a sigh of relief. She was alive. But the relief was quickly replaced by worry. "She's afraid. She's angry."

"Do you think she's still in Maine?" Silas asked, hopeful. Although I had been able to feel Athena from a vast distance before, there wasn't a doubt that I was feeling her too strongly now for her to be several states away.

"No," I responded, but I wasn't sure if that was good news or not. On one hand, when we finally broke out of here again, we wouldn't have to wait long for her to be back in our arms. On the other hand, she was a prisoner of Nameless just as we were, and who knows what vitriolic lies they were feeding her now.

"How did they find us so quickly?" Laz asked, defeatedly. I leaned my forehead against the cool metal bars.

"Maybe it was Louis? The missing person's case?" Samara offered, seemingly fully recovered from her initial shock of grief.

"Or maybe the ring of traffickers was too close. We should have gone further," Laz added.

"Did anyone see the symbol?" Silas asked, anger still lacing every word. He was seething with barely restrained fury. His shift would be close behind.

"No, nothing." Samara.

"I thought we had time." Laz.

"We can't dwell on that now," I stated, feeling their emotions shift to sadness. "We're here, and we can assume they have Athena." Three collective growls. I understood the impulse. I was going to tear the head off of any fucker who dared to put a hand on her perfect skin but in due time. She needed me to have a level head right now, but I admit that was getting harder with how strongly my coven emotions were slamming into me.

"They're going to regret this," Silas growled, an inhuman sound that told me he had shifted. His fangs were out, his skin was paler, his claws had elongated, and his eyes were blood-red. I could picture it clearly despite being unable to see him.

"Yes, they are," I agreed.

Deep in my chest, safe behind the layers of protection I had crafted, laid my bond with her. As if it were some tangible physical thing. I felt it there, burning brightly and offering me energy and power that I could only ever dream of before. It felt almost…enhanced. There were stories about mate bonds enhancing the latent power of vampires after completion, but so little has been studied that it was mere gossip and tall tales. But I felt it here. The connection with her was like a fiery inferno in the pit of my chest that was forging me into something better, something more substantial. I didn't know what it would mean or how it would manifest, but it was yet another advantage I hadn't factored into my plan and another thing the Hunters would never see coming. We weren't the same Wanderers that they held captive last time.

No, we have something even more vital to fight for this time. And something that's going to fight for us right back.

"What are we going to do?" Samara asked with a slight quiver in her voice.

"What we always do," I replied. "Survive."

ARCHER

THREE

My father never hugged me. It wasn't his thing. He's never been the touchy-feely kind of guy. Growing up, he would shake my hand when most parents would engage in some sort of physical connection with their children. So, it was incredibly jarring and strange to be in his embrace right now. His arms tightened around my shoulders, and he pulled me close to him—a slight chuckle in my ear. I patted him on the back once, twice. Entirely unsure how to react.

"I can't believe you did it, son," he said, pulling back from our embrace, his hands fixed on my shoulders painfully.

"Yep," I offered awkwardly.

"You have no idea what everyone's been saying. You're going to go down in history for this, Archer. Do you realize that?" His eyes glistened with the promise of fame that I never wanted.

"Sure." I shrugged.

His face fell. "What the hell is wrong with you?"

What was wrong with me? I didn't know. I wasn't exactly jazzed about becoming a Hunter, but I should be celebrating right now. I captured The Wanderers

Nameless' white whale. I did that. Alone. And yet… I didn't feel all that relieved.

"I just…"

He put a hand up. "Stop."

I watched him for a second. He pinched the bridge of his nose between his thumb and forefinger, and an exasperated sigh escaped his lips.

"You have been dragging your feet through life, son. You didn't start the academy until I forced you to." He groaned. "You wasted most of your life playing on that stupid guitar, and now that you've actually done something worthy with your life, you're acting like an ungrateful child."

I winced as his words found their mark. My father looked a lot like me. His eyes were a deep emerald, his hair a soft auburn color, the same as mine before I went and dyed over it. His toned muscles and his strong jawline were like mine, too. There was a time when I was his perfect mirror, and yet, there's a world of difference between the two of us.

"I did what you asked, Dad," I stated plainly. He nodded, letting loose a soft, incredulous chuckle.

"Yes, you did. Galvin is very impressed. He's going to expect big things from you from now on."

I simply watched him. I didn't know if I'd be able to respond in a way he'd deem acceptable. After a while, I broke the silence. "Where is Galvin?" I didn't want to run into him while roaming the halls randomly.

"He's been laying low for a while. A mission went south, and he had to hide until we could fix the situation." My father waved a hand in front of his face as if it wasn't a big deal to have the head of our underground vampire-hunting organization in hiding.

"And did you? Fix the situation?" I asked.

"Not yet, but Galvin assured me he is working on it."

I nodded, thankful that there wasn't a chance of an unexpected meeting with the frightening ruler of Nameless.

"What did you do with the human?" He asked.

The human.

Athena.

I hated how clinical it felt to talk about her. How little my father cared about what happened to her.

"She's in your office," I started. His eyes opened wide. "I didn't want to put blood that close to The Wanderers in the cells," I finished quickly, hoping that would placate him. It seemed to because he nodded.

"We'll have to interrogate her, figure out what she knows.' He began to pace in front of me. "She'll need to be analyzed. Figure out if she's an asset or a threat."

"And what if she's a threat?"

"You know we cannot operate without our anonymity, and if what you've told me is correct, she knows your face and real name." The thought stabbed me in the chest. Was Athena a threat because of how careless I had been?

"So what?" I prompted.

"Do you need me to say it?" He asked, an edge of disappointment in his tone.

"Yes, I want you to say it out loud. I want to hear you tell me what you would do to that innocent human being in there." I tried not to let my voice rise above a whisper, but the intensity was burning behind each word.

"She would need to die," he spoke so clearly, so confidently, like the words didn't make him sick. Like it wasn't a murder, he was suggesting.

"And if she's an asset?" There was only one way out of this for Athena, and I would do whatever it took to lead her down that path.

"She would join us."

I sucked in a sharp inhale. "You're kidding me. It's death or submission? Those are the options? Sounds an awful lot like this oppressive regime I've read about in my history books. You know, that guy was the villain, right," I spat sarcastically.

He almost responded when his phone buzzed in his pocket. As his eyes scanned the caller ID, he sighed and sent it to voicemail before retraining his eyes on me.

"We are in a war, Archer," he glowered. "People die in wars, and there is no happy ending for everybody."

"Right," I responded defeatedly. I knew I wouldn't win this battle with my father, and I couldn't focus on this anymore. I needed to figure out how to get Athena out of here with her life and freedom.

"Do I need to conduct this interrogation?" He asked.

"No," I replied. He nodded, scanning my form.

"You've made a great capture, kid. This wasn't a small feat, and people will not forget it. But even the tallest towers can be brought down by a single weak beam. So, don't make mistakes." He turned on his heel to head down the hallway, leaving me alone.

I sighed, glancing up at the door to his office and imagining the woman behind the door. She needed me to be innovative. She needed me to prove to her that those creatures were monsters. She needed to believe it.

And I knew just how to do it.

SAMARA
FOUR

Being in this cell even a few days ago might have killed me. Sensing Alora here, her pain, and her last few moments. Noticing the ghosts of her dancing in the corner and lurking in the shadows. The memory of her was so thick I was nearly choking on it. And I used to think that would be my downfall.

But despite the distance between us, I felt my mate holding my hand. Her soft touch on my face caressing it, encouraging me to wade through these troubled waters. With her grounding me, I could face these memories without losing myself.

It hurt being here, but instead of feeling Alora's death, I just felt her. And that made it all ok. Athena gave me that peace.

"You really think it will work?" Silas asked, his voice gruff. He had been entirely shifted for nearly the last hour. His anger was potent enough for me to feel it. I could only imagine what Orpheus was getting from him.

"I do," Orpheus responded casually. He was good in a crisis. While the others often praised my willpower, Orpheus usually held it together the most efficiently. If I didn't know him so well, I'd think he was completely fine with being back in Nameless' clutches. But I did know him, and I could tell how much being separated from Athena was hurting him. The sooner we put his plan into motion, the sooner we would be reunited with our mate, and the sooner we could finally get revenge on Nameless for all they've done to us and all they've taken away.

"We won't get very far if you're in a constant shift," Laz offered quietly.

"I can't help it," Silas growled.

"Let Athena help," I said softly. Athena wasn't a vampire, so she never bit us when we completed the bond. Which meant that we did not have a physical manifestation of our bond with her on our skin like she does with us. But she's still there in my soul. If I focused hard enough, I could feel that bond, visualize it, and follow it to her. She's there. She's always there. "Lean on her," I advised, doing the same. I traced the bond in my mind, hoping she could feel my passion for her in that mental touch. The others were quiet, no doubt trying to focus on that connection.

She made me feel strong—a better version of myself.

"It's gotta be convincing, Silas," Laz urged. Orpheus had a good plan, but Laz was right. If we couldn't pull it off, there was nothing else to do.

"They likely aren't going to hold us for long. They're not going to risk losing us again. So we've gotta start now," Orpheus reiterated. "I mean it. No matter what they throw at us, we take it. Ok?" I nodded.

The door at the end of the hall opened with a loud metallic clanging sound—a familiar, eerie sound that sent goosebumps across my flesh. It was time to put this plan into motion.

"Shift back, Silas, now," Orpheus ordered. I didn't have time to ask if he had done it.

The weight of footsteps was heavy, steadfast, and confident. As the man came into view, I knew immediately who he was, despite the mask covering his face. I would know his frame anywhere. The last time I saw him, he was driving a stake through my wife's heart. Fury bubbled under the surface of my skin. It took every ounce of the willpower I had to remain calm.

He stopped several feet behind the red line and clasped his hands before him.

"Hello, Wanderers." The sound of his voice was grating, like nails on a chalkboard. It ground against my soul. "I see you've made yourselves right at home."

I could practically hear the smug smirk on his face behind the mask.

"Bennett, right?" Orpheus asserted. I gripped the bars and watched his body language carefully. He tensed at that. They never expected us to escape the last time, so they got careless and let some of their anonymity slip. Not enough. There are a million Bennetts in this state. I couldn't find him without a first name. And I tried. We all tried for a long time. It wasn't enough to find him outside these walls, but it was enough to throw him off balance here. And that's the advantage we needed.

"Hmm," he stood calmly as if he weren't facing off against four ferocious vampires. We've been preparing for your return to us." His shrouded eyes scanned each of us; it felt like a violation, his gaze on me.

"So have we," Orpheus retorted with a smirk—all part of the plan.

"You know, the Hunter who captured you mentioned that you've been out in the sunlight." He leaned back against the empty cells on the opposite side of the hall from us with a casual, taunting attitude. "That's a fun new little development."

There was a vampire living in New Orleans who was rumored to have the ability to make it so that vampires could exist in the daylight. It was a heavily guarded secret and an even more heavily guarded vampire. Her compound was acres upon acres of guards and traps. It took us a whole year to convince her to see us and a few months after that to persuade her to perform the ritual on us. It was only when we told her our story that she truly listened. As it turned out, she had lost someone to Nameless' clutches, too—her husband. Unfortunately, or fortunately, depending on how you look at it, the man she described was none other than the man who was two cages down from us when we arrived. The man who had all but given up. She asked about him. We told her the truth. She cried. We cried. Eventually, she performed the ritual. It was painful like she was burning our body from the inside out, but when it was done and we stepped out onto the lawn of her manor, feeling the rays of light for the first time in a century, or in Orpheus's case, even longer, I couldn't help the tears that fell.

She made us promise to use this new ability to our advantage. We swore we would.

"Are you waiting for me to tell you how we did it?" Orpheus asked, provoking him.

"Would you tell the truth?" Bennett asked with a slight chuckle.

"Unlike you, Bennett, I'm not hiding what I am."

Bennett's hands tensed at his side. "So what is it? Complete immunity? Or is there a threshold?"

We stayed quiet. He laughed. "Of course there is." He moved to a lever on the wall. I immediately noticed it was not there the last time we were here. I would know because I'd memorized every inch of these walls. "Are you going to tell me what that threshold is, or should we find it together?"

Before Orpheus had a chance to respond, Bennett flipped the lever. A loud mechanical whirring filled the air, and I cringed at how overwhelming the sound felt to my advanced hearing. I looked up to see that the ceiling of the cell was sliding back to reveal a clear pane of glass and a blistering sun. The light flooded into every corner of the cell, chasing every last shadow away. The rays hit my skin, searing. I stifled a cry.

I heard my companions cry out as the sun's rays assaulted them.

The sun burned it a way it hadn't since before the ritual. My flesh felt tender and raw under its heat. I tried to fold over myself, hiding my uncovered skin, but there was no reprieve from the blistering warmth.

"That glass above you? It's specially designed to enhance the sun's rays."

I winced as the heat burned through the clothes on my back. I pressed against the walls, trying to find the slightest shade, but there was no hiding from the burn. Every inch of the cell was basked in shining vicious light. And it charred my skin.

Tears stung my eyes, but I endured the torture. I would not let this monster see me fall apart. He didn't deserve the satisfaction.

I felt like I was being flayed open, laid bare beneath the blazing inferno. My skin was so warm I felt like it might burst into flames any instant. There's something so vulnerable about being betrayed by your own skin. In the last few years, I'd come to appreciate the sun's warmth again. We weren't immune to its light, but the pain was minimal in comparison.

I heard Silas let out a string of curses, and Laz stifled a scream. Orpheus was stoic and silent as usual, but I could feel their injuries, the way the fiery sun was assaulting their skin and violently blistering their bodies. Shock filled me then when I realized just how intimately I could feel them, in fact. Fully and completely. I could see the burns and sense the edges of the blisters. I could feel them as strongly as I could if I were touching them. Despite the burning light that was still viciously licking at my sensitive skin, I felt hope.

My entire body was in pain, stinging, violent pain. It felt like a thousand needles were prickling at me, but I focused on this new development of my power—this latest extension of myself. Eventually, the pain was numbing, and the light receded as Bennett flipped the lever back.

Silas felt it most in his hands, which he had used to shield his face. The palms were raw and tender. His arms were faring not much better. Laz, like me, had attempted to shield from the rays by folding over themselves, so their back had gotten the worst of it. Orpheus' face was the part that burnt the most for him, as if he had stood his ground, refusing to shy away from this display of torture.

I let my mind analyze their injuries, study them, and embrace them. I'd never been able to do anything like this before. The excitement flooding me was nearly enough to overshadow the unbearable pain that was radiating through my body from the assault.

"You've got new tricks, but so do we," Bennett said before leaving the hall. I watched him go, and once we heard the tell-tale lock at the door, I listened to my companions truly let the weight of that settle on them.

"Fuck, I'd almost forgotten how bad that fucking hurts," Silas seethed. I let my mind focus on his hands. The palms. Red and angry.

"We're not going to have to pretend to let the torture weaken us if it's all like that," Laz whispered meekly. Their back was throbbing in my mind.

"We'll manage," Orpheus said through clenched teeth, no doubt trying to hold back the wave of emotion he had held so tightly to his chest. He tried to remain calm for us, tried to be strong. However, I knew he felt our pain. Each of us was forced to live our own pain while he lived all of ours as well as his own. The involuntary waves of our agony always found their way to him. He hid it well, how much that affected him, but I knew how hard that was for him. Feeling the injury deep in his skin, I let my gift sweep over his face.

If I could feel their injuries from this far… maybe... Just maybe.

I focused on the burns, one at a time, letting every ounce of my ability pour through the connections my mind had made to their worst wounds. It felt strange, an entirely new sensation, but no less powerful. It flowed through the channels of my mind, finding purchase on their burns, seeping into their skin, cooling them from within, calming the angry burns, urging the skin to reform. It was harder to navigate, but within seconds, I felt the burns disappear from their flesh, and their injuries fell away. Only then did I let my healing wash over myself.

"What the fuck?" Silas asked incredulously.

"How did-" Laz.

"Samara," Orpheus interjected. "Did you just-"

"A bond makes us stronger," I whispered, feeling the last remnants of the sting recede from my skin.

"Holy shit," Silas exclaimed. "No fucking way."

"Are you all ok?" I asked.

"Like it never fucking happened," Silas responded excitedly.

"I feel fine, perfectly fine," Laz said with a laugh.

"Are you drained?" Orpheus whispered eagerly.

"Not at all," I replied, taking stock of my current state. If anything, I felt stronger than before. More resolved.

"This changes everything," Laz added, and hope laced every word.

"Yes, it does," Orpheus said, and I could hear the smirk playing on his lips. I looked down at myself. My dress was tattered and torn, and the edges were seared from the fire that was nearly flaming on my body just moments ago.

"Can you feel her?" Silas asked. "Is she hurt?" I steadied my breathing and closed my eyes. Focusing my power on my mate. She was far enough away that it wasn't as easy of a task as it was for me to feel my coven, but after a few moments of intense focus, I found her. Her influence felt like a salve, a reward, every good thing I'd missed for many years. She was mine.

"There she is," I whispered.

"Is she ok?" Laz asked.

I let my power wash over her body, analyzing her pain and injuries. Her body had taken some hits, a contusion on her head, and her throat and shoulders were bruised. Long and thick bruises formed on her back as if she was slammed into something repeatedly. But the worst part was her hands. They were swollen, and tiny cuts danced along the knuckles. It was evident that she had to use them to defend herself. A growl escaped my lips.

"She's hurt," I seethed.

"Heal her," Silas urged angrily.

"Wait," Orpheus interjected before I let my power flow through the connection.

"What do you mean, wait?" Silas argued.

"We are vampires, so our skin healing won't make them suspicious," he started. "But Athena is human. If her injuries suddenly disappear, they're going to notice. We'd lose this advantage, or worse, they'd think she was one of us somehow."

I cursed under my breath. He was right.

"Can you relieve the pain but leave the outward facade of injuries?" He asked.

I'd never tried to do anything like that before. Why would I have?

"I'm not sure," I answered truthfully, trying to keep my focus on each of the vicious little injuries that littered her body.

"Try," Orpheus demanded in a soft, almost pleading sort of way. The thought of her in pain was agonizing, but the idea of putting her under unnecessary scrutiny in this place was worse.

I zeroed in on her internal pain, trying my hardest to ignore the outward bruises and wounds despite how my power itched to erase those from marring her perfect skin. Letting my ability wash over her felt like taking a long, languid breath of fresh air after being locked inside somewhere stifling. She felt like a relief, like the moment of calm at the end of a dangerous ride. I smiled and let my power get to work. I imagined kissing her skin and taking the pain away. If I couldn't press my lips to her skin, at least I could do this.

With each rush of my power, I felt her pain recede slowly but effectively. It pained me to leave those cuts untouched, to let the bruises on her back remain, but I took solace in the fact that she wasn't in pain anymore.

That's when I felt her. Stronger than before.

Thank you, Samara.

Her whispered words felt like they were spoken directly into my ear, so much so that my eyes sprung open, and I turned in hopes of catching a glimpse of her, but she wasn't there. I whispered back through the channels of my mind.

Athena?

I waited a moment, then another. Finally, her voice returned.

Samara? Can you hear me? Is this real, or am I hallucinating?

I giggled.

"What is it?" Orpheus asked. I pressed against the bars of my cell and smiled brightly for the first time since waking up in this hell.

"Have you ever heard of mates being able to speak telepathically?" I asked, focusing then on the bond.

It's real, sweetheart. It's me.

I heard her sigh.

"No," Orpheus responded.

Are you all ok? Athena asked.

She was in pain, and yet she asked about us, her mates. My heart thumped once, firmly against my chest.

We will be when we get you out of here. I offered back to her.

"She's talking to me now." I heard Silas and Laz gasp.

"So little is known about multiple mates. Perhaps it's got something to do with that?" Laz offered. I shrugged, although they couldn't see me.

What can I do to help?

I shook my head. *Stay safe and alive.*

"What is she saying?" Silas begged.

"She's asking how she can help," I said, pride lacing my tone.

You too. Thank you for kissing it better.

My chest warmed in that love-filled way, a vastly different heat than the sun that had just torn through my skin.

I wanted to respond, to tell her that I wasn't 'alive,' but ever since she came into my life, she had been making me experience life in a way I never thought I'd be able to again. I may not be alive, but Athena made me want to be, and that was enough.

"We're going to get out of here," Orpheus said, determined and clear. I had heard him say those exact words a dozen times the last time we were here.

But when he said them this time, I actually believed him.

ATHENA

FIVE

It felt like warm honey spreading through my entire body. I could feel her healing powers take hold of the pain that was throbbing in my limbs and my chest and wipe it away.

I don't know how, but I could speak to her through that bond that thrummed so powerfully inside my chest. Over the next day, or maybe longer, I tried to establish the same line of communication with each of them with little success. I hadn't even been able to reestablish the link with Samara. Suddenly, I felt even more lonely than before. I didn't know how heavy the toll of their loss was on my soul until I heard Samara's voice. And I wouldn't be able to settle until I could speak to them all and hear directly from their lips that they were okay.

Well, as 'okay' as anyone could be when trapped.

The door creaked open, scratching the wooden floor below violently, and I cringed. Light flooded into the room, sending wicked shadows sprawling across the floor. As my eyes adjusted, a silhouette came into view.

My heart rate sped up as I saw them.

"I told you I didn't want to talk to you," I spat as Archer entered the room, closing the door behind him.

"I need you to understand why I did this, Athena," he pleaded. He looked tired as if he hadn't slept in days. Well good, I hope he never sleeps again.

"Understand why you've kidnapped me? And my mates?"

His eyes burned with shock. "They cannot be your mates, Athena."

"Fuck you," I growled, the words slipping out in an animalistic possessive way. Archer ran a hand down his face and stopped a few feet from me. I noticed the bulky file folder in his hands for the first time.

"I'm not the monster here," he said, letting the file fall to the table to the side. He opened it, and papers spilled out across the surface of the desk. I tried to fight my curiosity and ignore his apparent attempt to goad me, but my eyes drifted toward the documents nevertheless.

What I saw was unimaginable.

Pictures, reports, and statements. Mangled bodies, blood-stained skin, and clothing puncture wounds deep into their throats. The pale, lifeless figures stared up at me from the pages, and I watched them in horror. Death. So much death on these pages.

I felt bile rise in my throat, and I forced myself to look away from the images. I heard rustling but refused to turn back to Archer.

"I'm sorry," Archer started quietly. "I didn't want to upset you, but you needed to understand what we're trying to prevent here."

I looked at him tentatively to see that he had filed away the photos.

"Who were those people?" I asked, meekly and unsure if I even wanted the answer.

"Victims," he replied. I shook my head. I was trying to piece together the jumbled mess of information flowing through my mind.

"My mates aren't like that," I asserted, confident but shaky in my conviction. He lifted the folder and turned it so I could see the labeled tab. Two words were printed along the top. Two words that stole my breath and clenched my heart. Two words and the world changed.

The Wanderers.

I gasped and felt tears sting my eyes. "No, no. They…" I struggled to find my breath. "They only kill monsters, people who hurt others." It was what they told me. And I believed them. I believed every word. Louis had been trying to hurt me. That's why he ended up the way he did.

A look crossed Archer's face, which looked a lot like pity, and he flipped open the folder. He took a deep breath and slid an image from the confines of the folder. With a deep breath, he turned it toward him. The woman in the photo was small young, maybe mid-twenties at most. Her soft brown hair was messy and sprawled on the concrete floor beneath her body. Her lifeless eyes stared into nothingness, and the blood that coated her shoulder was deep crimson. The two puncture wounds were vicious and angry-looking. I tried to avert my eyes, but I couldn't seem to look away from her.

"This is Lily Anders, a kindergarten teacher in Kentucky. She just turned twenty-four when she was murdered."

I swallowed the lump in my throat as Archer set the photo down and pulled another. The older man was dressed in a business suit. His wrinkled black skin was ashen, his eyes glazed and dead. The puncture wounds on his throat taunted me.

"Victor Brown, a civil rights activist from Montgomery, Alabama. He marched in The Selma Marches in the '60s and the women's liberation arches in the '70s. He survived all that only to die by the fangs of The Wanderers."

A soft sob fell from my lips as he discarded that photo and reached for another. The couple in the picture took my breath away. She wore a gorgeous white gown, painted and marred by the blood that ran from the puncture wounds on her neck. Her groom was discarded before her, his arms twisted unnaturally as he lay there. Their hands froze on the ground as if reaching for each other, even in death.

"Violet and Zander Freedman married just four hours before they were killed. They had a two-year-old at home."

Another photo.

Another story.

"Jennifer Kaufman, foster mother of 4." He slammed the photo down onto the desk. "George Haroldson, special education teacher. Bethany Terrison, Olympic hopeful." The photos fell from his grasp onto the desk, and I could no longer contain my sobs. "Francessca Dodson, ten years old." He held that photo in front of me for longer than the others. A look of pain on his face as he watched me take it all in.

'Stop," I cried, forcing my eyes to look away from the small frame in the photo before me. My head hung forward, and tears fell down my cheeks in steady streams. I heard Archer shuffle about, and then he was kneeling before me, his hands-free from the file.

"Did those people look like monsters to you?" He asked it so gently, as if the tone of his question could soften the pain in my chest.

It didn't.

I shook my head, sobbing. Archer reached for my shoulder, and I shied away from his touch. He pulled back, looking ashamed and guilty.

"I'm sorry," he stated. "That was… I just. I needed you to understand how dangerous they are, Athena. I can save a lot of lives by killing them."

I cried out, pain radiating through every nerve in my body at the thought of losing any of my mates and what they might be capable of.

"You're so lucky, Athena," he began, and I scoffed. "They could have bitten you. They could have killed you." I shook my head.

"They did," I whispered. His eyebrows furrowed.

"What do you mean?"

"They did bite me," I answered weakly, remembering the moment their fangs pierced my skin and laid claim to my heart, body, and soul. Tainted now by Archer's demonstration.

Archer's eyes scanned my throat and then my arms frantically.

"No…" he started.

"They wouldn't do those things," I whispered to him, knowing with every fiber of who I am that they were not responsible for the evil acts harbored within that file. "They wouldn't."

"But they did," he pleaded, his eyes begging with me. I shook my head.

"You said they bit you?" He asked, looking at my throat again. I nodded, hating the way he made it sound like a death sentence or something to be afraid of when it was the most beautiful experience of my life. "Where?"

"My throat, chest, hip, and wrist."

He sat back on his heels, looking at the image now painted on my skin.

"Those markings…" he whispered. I nodded again.

"The mate bond."

He shook his head, muttering under his breath. "There would be puncture wounds." A thought occurred to me then, a memory that seemed so distant now.

"The saliva in a vampire bite counteracts the wound," I whispered as the revelation came.

"What?" Archer asked from his position on his knees before me.

"A vampire's saliva counteracts the wound, closes it up." I felt a bloom of hope in my chest. "Those photos all had the bite, clear as day. That's not my Wanderers." I was ashamed that it took me this long to put it together.

"That's not possible," he stammered, but I saw the slightest edge of suspicion in his eyes.

"Archer," I said, trying to catch his eyes. He looked up at me, and for the first time since I realized what he had done, I saw the same Archer who was my friend with soft green eyes and tender gaze. "I am not lying to you. I was bitten. Their saliva closed my wounds. They do not leave punctures like that." I gestured to the file that sat on the floor by his knees. "I don't know who killed those people, Archer, but it wasn't them," I remembered back to the unspoken rule they told me about. "It probably wasn't a vampire at all."

He shook his head, disgust coloring his features. "You're brainwashed, do you even hear yourself?" he stood and paced around the room. "Saliva magically closing a bite? Are you kidding me?" He ran his hands through his hair.

"We can prove it."

He turned back to me, his eyes wild.

"Let them bite me. They'll show you."

He laughed a sort of crazed chuckle, disbelief pouring from him. "They would kill you, Athena! Don't you see that? They are trapped here and haven't fed for two days. They would drain you completely!"

I shook my head. "They won't."

He tossed his hands up in defeat. "You're unbelievable. How far have they gotten their hooks in you?" He dug into the file, sliding the pictures around till his hand found the one he wanted.

When he turned the picture to face me, I felt a sickening twist deep in my abdomen. Louis' smiling face looked up at me. The photo looked like it was a few months old. His hair was shorter than it was that night at the Craving Crab. I visibly shied away from the photo.

"They killed him, didn't they? The missing guy?"

I looked up at him, hating the way his figure blurred in my vision from the tears that were forming. I didn't respond.

"They did. They did it," he confirmed from my silence. "How can you defend them, Athena? They are murderers, monsters!"

"Louis tried to rape me!" I screamed. My throat was raw, and I hated the way the word felt on my tongue, like ash and death. Archer's eyes softened, and a sharp exhale spilled from his lips at my confession.

"What?" he asked, nearly under his breath.

"Louis drugged my drink and took me outside of the bar," I started, feeling the weight of the memory settling on my chest. "He had my underwear down, and he was about to... He was almost.." A sob fell from my lips as I tried to compose myself. "But then they found me, they saved me. They *saved* me, Archer. The only monster in that alleyway was Louis."

"No…" he whispered, and just one word was enough to shatter my composure. He didn't believe me. Of course, he didn't believe me. No one ever did.

"Please…They aren't the villains here."

He glared at me, a mixture of disbelief and anger on his face, before turning to leave the room.

"Wait, Archer, please!" I called after him. He paused but didn't turn back to face me. "You may not believe me, but I'm telling you the truth."

"Athena…" he started.

"One of us is going to be wrong about this. Please just… consider that it might be you."

His shoulders rose and fell as he took a deep breath before exiting the room and leaving me alone in the darkness again.

SILAS

SIX

Samara's healing powers helped relieve the pain of the burns but not the memory of their sting. It had been a while since I considered the sun a weapon. I hated how quickly I had forgotten. How easily I fell back into the mindset of humanity. The sun was the hardest goodbye I had to make when I was turned. I had no family besides Alora, and she turned with me. I didn't have many friends or prospects, so the one thing I honestly had to give up was sunlight.

At first, being thrust into darkness felt like a payment I was willing to make, but after months, then years, then decades of surviving only at night…it began to take its toll.

Being gifted the ability to survive in sunlight again was the only thing that helped hold me together after losing Alora. Knowing how much she would have loved to feel the rays on her face again hurt, so despite the slight burn, I would sit outside and feel her there with me.

To have it ripped away again so brutally, fucking sucked.

I couldn't wait for the day that I got to sink my fangs into Bennett's throat

Earth for another moment, but I would wait until the time was right.

"Two weeks is too long," I whined, leaning my head against the cold metal bars of my enclosure.

"If we act any sooner, they will expect us to be full strength," Orpheus added. I hated how cocky he sounded, although I knew he was right. "We need to give it enough time for them to think we're weak."

I nodded, sighing.

"That will be too long to be away from her," Samara whispered. I knew what she meant. My soul was also crying for Athena.

"She's strong, and we must be strong for her too." Orpheus' tone was laced with love. There was a time I'd never thought I'd hear him speak about another person like that. He was always so solitary. Even in our coven, he found his reasons to be alone, to isolate himself. Feeling everyone else's emotions constantly can't be easy, so I never blamed him. It was hard, though, to see how lonely he was. If you had told me a year ago that he'd be helplessly head over heels, for a human no less, I would have laughed. But Athena changed everything when she walked into our lives. I saw how she had started healing wounds in Laz, Samara, and Orpheus that were so old and deep that they'd all but given up on feeling whole again. She was mending us, she saw our scars, and instead of shying away or trying to hide them away, she kissed them and told us we deserved the happiness she promised. Samara, Laz, and Orpheus deserved that.

"So we have a timeline," Laz started. "And a plan."

I nodded along. It was a good plan. Orpheus clearly had put a lot of thought into our inevitable need to escape from here again, and the plan has only become more solid with the development of Samara's gift. Orpheus hinted that his gift might have progressed as well, although he wasn't sure exactly what the nature of it was now. Laz and I, however, felt entirely…the same. Not anymore powerful than we had before. Which was fine by me. I didn't join my soul with Athena's for some supernatural upgrade. However, Orpheus is convinced that new skills can still develop over time.

"Do we finally want to discuss theories as to why we're all mated to Athena?" Laz whispered, but we could hear them clearly.

"It doesn't matter," I said, probably a little too forcefully, instantly regretting how harsh I had sounded.

"I know, but it certainly is interesting. Considering it's so rare," they continued, ignoring my outburst. I was thankful for that. I knew they hadn't meant offense.

"Any chance one of you is vampire royalty and forgot to tell us?" I joked with a soft chuckle.

"The monarchy hasn't had an heir," Orpheus began. The royal family was more 'for show' than anything else. Our King has held the throne for nearly two centuries. His Queen was killed before I was even born as a human, and as far as any of us know, he hasn't created an heir.

"Could be illegitimate," I added unhelpfully. To create an 'heir,' a vampire must drink the human nearly dry before allowing them to feed on the vamp's blood. Then, after the transformation, the fresh-turn must drink first from the vamp who created them. It solidifies some sort of preternatural bond. No one is naive enough to think the King has never made another vampire, but there's never been a purposeful heir as far as anyone knows.

"So, short of being a bastard child of the royal line, the other multiple mate covens have been vamps with indescribable power," Orpheus added.

"We're all fairly powerful," Samara interjected.

"Yes, but not in comparison to these other covens. We're talking vampires with the ability to alter time and space," Orpheus continued. I had heard him talk about those gifts before. There was still so much I didn't know about my new existence. That's what happens when you're on the run.

"There's time-traveling vampires?" Laz whispered incredulously.

"There were," Orpheus replied solemnly. "Most of them have been hunted."

"How do you kill a time-traveling vamp? Couldn't they just keep rewinding until they escaped?" I asked.

"It's foolish to assume that the Hunters haven't considered countermeasures for most of our gifts."

I sighed, feeling anger course through my veins. Those Hunters have created such a horrific state of fear in our community. I couldn't wait for the day that we finally end them once and for all.

"Maybe we're not the powerful ones?" Samara whispered.

"You think Athena is?" Laz asked incredulously, but I could tell they were genuinely considering it.

"She's the common denominator here. She could have an extremely powerful latent vampire gift." Samara spoke so quietly as not to alert the guards or cameras of her theory.

"If that's true, we can't even allow the Hunters to consider it," Orpheus returned forcefully. "Who knows what lengths they'll go to to "study" our kind."

The thought of Athena being turned into a vampire sent a weird swirl of emotions through my chest. On the one hand, I wanted to spend eternity with her, and I wanted to live my life without worrying about her growing old, without worrying about her mortal form and how vulnerable she was. On the other, this life - although it was my salvation - is a curse, and it would be foolish of me to think of it any other way. I wouldn't wish this life on anyone who hasn't thoroughly prepared for what it meant.

"They're trying to eradicate us. They wouldn't make a new one," Laz started. "Would they?"

"We cannot trust their words, only their actions," Orpheus replied, his voice laced with fear. We've seen firsthand what sort of 'actions' these Hunters perform. "Think about it. They held us captive for over two months. We were weak, fucking inches from desiccating. If they wanted to kill us, they could have. So why didn't they?" He asked.

"Because they're looking for something else…" Samara finished.

"Exactly."

We were quiet for a moment. What could they be looking for? What could they learn by torturing us within an inch of existence? What would they do to Athena?

"I want to destroy them," I said, finally breaking the silence. Laz grunted in agreement.

"We need to focus on getting out of here," Orpheus said calmly.

"And then what?" I spat. "If we get out of here, where do we go? Do you want us to run forever?"

He didn't respond.

"Athena won't leave her grandma or Davia. She won't go on the run with us, Orpheus. She shouldn't have to."

"The Hunters will never stop," Orpheus pleaded.

"Then we stop them! Here and now. I'm tired of running, aren't you?" A tense quiet fell over us. My breathing slowed as I waited for him to respond.

"Of course I am." It was a whisper. Defeated. Ashamed. "But I can't risk it. I can't lose any more family."

I inhaled sharply at the confession.

"I don't know what to do." It was an admission that we had never heard from his lips. Orpheus, the leader of our coven, had always known what to do. He was the man with the plan. To hear him so defeated, so lost…well, it was a perfect example of how fucking dangerous this whole thing was. We fucking barely escaped last time. Even with Samara and Orpheus' new potential powers, getting out alive will be a challenge. Let alone take the Hunters down in the process.

I let my head rest on the metal bars of my cage, wishing I could replace their harsh touch with that of my mate. Two weeks was too long, but I knew without a doubt that I would make up for every second of lost time the moment she was in my arms again.

ARCHER

SEVEN

My head was spinning when I sat down at the bar. The dive was a staple for us Hunters, as it was the only establishment within twenty miles of our little operation. The Wooden Stake was owned and operated by Hunters, of course. Who else would be stupid enough to name a place, The Wooden Stake? The moment I stepped inside, I was enveloped in an atmosphere that immediately transported me to another time and place. The main area is a dimly lit, cozy chamber adorned with dark wood and heavy velvet curtains that hang in thick folds, muffling sounds and adding an air of secrecy. Antique weapons and hunting paraphernalia adorned the walls, from wooden stakes to silver-bladed weapons, each telling a story of battles against the undead and unnatural. I did not come here often, but I needed a drink and a clear head tonight. It had been nearly a week since I stopped in to speak with Athena. Someone else had been tasked with bringing her meals, although I've been informed she was not eating. I wanted to go in there and convince her to believe me, to trust me, but I just couldn't get her words out of my head.

I glanced around the dimly lit room. The patrons come from all walks of life

Some were seasoned hunters, bearing scars and grim determination etched into their faces, while others were newcomers seeking guidance. The bartender was a Hunter I didn't recognize, but I saw the raised white scar from the brand on his forearm. I didn't know how to make sense of the feeling I got when I looked at it. There was an almost sickening apprehension building in the pit of my stomach. The scent of burnt flesh was still so visceral in my memory.

"What can I get ya, kid?"

I narrowly resisted rolling my eyes at the belittling honorific. I may not have recognized the bartender, but there was an excellent chance he would have recognized me—Son of the great Jacob Bennett.

"Whiskey rocks, please."

With a nod, he turned to get my drink, and I stared at his back. He wore a tank top showcasing his ridiculous muscles, which was probably his desired effect. It also showcased the bite marks that decorated his skin. Several deep and angry white scars stood out against his olive skin. As he poured the drink, I studied those scars. Two deep puncture wounds, flanked on each side by several thin pinpricks from the vamps, additional sharpened teeth. His scars looked a lot like mine. Mindlessly, I ran my thumb across the marred flesh at my wrist.

Athena claimed that vampire bites could be closed. Then why do we all carry these scars? Why is my skin forever marked from that day? Why did my father, this bartender, and so many other Hunters have bites decorating their skin?

I shook my head. What was it that Athena had claimed? A vampire's saliva. How did she expect me to believe that? Well, it's not like the Hunters would give a vampire a chance to lick the wound.

Not that it would do anything if they did.

"Starting a tab?" He asked. I shook my head and tossed some bills down on the counter. He grabbed them and strolled away to help the other Hunters on the far end of the bar.

The first sip of the drink sent a warm rush through my entire body. A few sips later, I felt my phone vibrating violently in my pocket. With a sigh, I reached for the phone.

The name on the caller ID screen had my blood turning cold, erasing any ounce of warmth I had just felt.

DAVIA

"Fuck," I cursed, sitting up straighter and glancing around at the other patrons. Other than the bartender, there were four other people here. Two Hunters were seated at the far end of the bar, and two more were sitting at a table by the jukebox. Fleetwood Mac played through the bar, masking any conversations the others were having. If I couldn't hear them, they wouldn't be able to hear me. Right?

My hand gripped the phone tensely. A sheen of sweat formed on my brow bone. I considered sending it to voicemail. Strongly. But something told me Davia wouldn't be deterred so easily.

Had she realized Athena was gone? It had been over a week.

I cleared my throat and answered the call.

"Well, well, well, did you miss me?" I answer, trying to interject the same charm I usually had with her.

"Have you seen Athena?" She was all business; her voice had no edge of accusation, but I knew she was only calling because she thought I might know something. I took a deep breath and relied on every ounce of training I'd ever had.

"She didn't tell you?" I began. I had to skip town. I left about a week and a half ago. I hope to make it back for one of those summer concerts, though. She invited me." It took all my energy to keep my voice calm and steady.

"When did you last see her?" Davia demanded.

"Whoa, what's going on? Is she ok?" I asked, feeling a twinge of guilt grip my chest.

"She's missing," Davia answered, her voice wavering briefly, unable to contain her fear and worry. I hated how I was the cause of that pain. I swallowed the lump in my throat and refocused on the task at hand.

"What the fuck? Since when?" I laced my voice with as much worry as I could.

"Nine days now."

I didn't miss how her voice caught, full-on an emotion she was too afraid to share.

"Have you gone to the police?" I asked carefully.

"Yeah, they are concerned that.. um... " She held back a sob, composing herself. "They're concerned that Greg has something to do with it." There was so much guilt in her voice. "They've tried to find him, but he's missing too. He hasn't been back to his rental. They think he... They think he might have taken her." A full sob escaped her lips then, and I let my head fall forward into my free hand.

Moral dilemmas were becoming more and more frequent lately. Having the police consider Greg was perfect for many reasons. It kept them from looking at me and gave them a trail to follow. BI could tell that Davia already felt so much guilt from introducing Athena to that douche's friend for her to think he was behind her disappearance and that it was all her fault was almost too much for me to bear. Almost.

"I knew I shouldn't have left town until that asshole was behind bars for what he did to her." I heard Davia sniffle on the other end of the call. "Just, um, let me know if you hear anything, ok?" She pleaded so helplessly.

"Of course," I promised, but it tasted like ash on my tongue.

I tried to view the situation as if I were hearing it all for the first time. What would I say if I didn't know exactly where Athena was?

"Have you tried talking to those people she was seeing?" I asked as evenly as I could.

"They're not in town either. Their rental was tossed, and windows were broken in. Cops aren't sure what to make of it all," she finished with a defeated tone.

"Shit," I whispered, trying my best to ignore the treacherous guilt that was threatening to eat me alive. "Are you ok?" I asked, knowing the answer.

"Of course I'm not okay. My best friend is missing, and it's my fault," she bit.

"Don't say that," I interject.

"Why not?" She asked, sniffling again. "It's the truth. I asked her to come out that night, and if I didn't make her go, or if I didn't leave her to go hook up if I was a better person… literally none of this would have happened." She cried softly, anger laced her words.

"Davia, come on, that is not true," I offered quickly. "If Greg is behind this, then it's nobody's fault but his." The words felt vitriolic in my mouth.

It's nobody's fault but mine.

She was quiet for a few moments, and I could tell she didn't care for that logic right now.

"Just let me know if you hear anything," she said sharply before hanging up. The silence on the other end of the call was the loudest thing I'd ever heard.

Shoving the phone back into my pocket, I grabbed my glass and downed the rest of my drink in one gulp. I begged the warmth of the liquor to thaw the cold, eerie guilt that had blanketed me, but it didn't.

The stool next to mine was pulled back, and I saw a figure sitting down out of the corner of my eye. He slid his phone onto the bar and reached for his wallet.

"You don't normally come here," my father said as he waved over the bartender. I didn't turn to look at him and watched as the muscled man behind the bar brought him a gin and tonic. When my father had his drink, I felt his eyes burn into my cheek, but I didn't turn to meet his gaze.

"It's been over a week. Have you made any progress with the girl?" He asked casually, but I knew better. He probably had tracked me down to ask this specific question.

I didn't want to tell him how difficult she was being. I wasn't sure what he might do to her if he learned she wasn't budging. A few weeks ago, I'd say we would let her go. But now? I'm not sure my father would be willing to let her go, knowing all she does. That thought sent a confusing feeling to my heart.

"Slow but steady," I replied, opting for vagueness.

"Does she know the truth about vampires?" He asked, taking a swig of his drink.

There it was. Moment of truth. Was I going to lie to my father to save her life? Or was I going to betray her and sentence her to death? I felt my hand tremble as I motioned for the bartender to pour me another drink.

"You ever heard of a vampire bite closing up? With like saliva or something?" I tried to say it with as little interest as possible. He took another drink, and I turned my head just enough to gauge his reaction. My father was skilled at hiding things, his emotions mostly, so I didn't see much of a response on his face. But as good as he was at hiding, I was just as good at reading. I learned from him, after all.

"That's the type of question someone asks when they let delusions win," he answered finally.

"Not delusions, Dad. I'm just curious," I respond as the bartender slides another drink before me.

"Did that girl say something?" He asked, an almost imperceptible sliver of worry gracing his features.

"No, I was doing some research," I replied evenly. My father made a slight humming sound and took another drink.

"Why the hell would you be looking into something like that, kid?" He seethed. "You know as well as I do that vampire bites do not disappear." He gripped my wrist and held it up so that I could see the scar. I pulled my arm from his hand and bit my lip.

"I'm not a kid." My eyes met his. This time, I wasn't backing down. His eyes narrowed, and he clicked his tongue before turning and taking another drink. His phone vibrated on the bar. The caller ID read *Carmen*. He quickly sent the call to voicemail and slid the phone back into his pocket. His jaw was tense, and I felt his body go rigid next to mine.

Who the hell is Carmen?

"Right," he mused quietly, moving on without addressing the call. "So the girl. She gonna be a problem?"

I couldn't help but sigh, a soft, incredulous chuckle falling from my lips.

"What's so funny?" He asked.

"I just can't believe this is my life sometimes," I answered finally, looking over at him and taking a long sip from my drink.

"Protecting the human race from monsters?" He asked, an edge of arrogance lacing his tone.

"Treating an innocent human like she's a threat," I bit back softly. I was resisting the urge to bolt out of the bar.

"She is a threat," my dad said calmly. I had always seen this man as my hero. The man who was protecting humans from the creatures of the night. The man who would save us all. Now, as he sat before me and tipped the amber liquid to his lips, I saw a liar. How many innocent people have been caught in his crossfire in this unending desire to eradicate vampires? Does he care?

"Right."

I shook my head and took another drink, downing the rest of the liquid in one gulp. I let the burn calm my ever-growing suspicion. Questioning things can get you killed here.

"Do I need to remove you from this case, Archer?" He asked coldly.

For a brief moment, I entertained the thought of leaving Athena and this mind-fucking case behind me. Shoving it onto someone else's plate to worry about. The only reason I was so confused and conflicted was because I got to know Athena. I wouldn't care as much if she remained a stranger. It would have been easier if she was someone else's problem.

But the thought of my father, or one of the other vicious Hunters, back at Nameless getting their hands on her and sinking their brand into her skin made my blood begin to boil.

"No, I've got it. I've established a rapport. You'd have to start all over with someone new."

He seemed to like that answer.

"What are you doing with The Wanderers?" The question tumbled out of my mouth before I could stop it. His eyes scanned the bar for any listening ears.

"Testing their limits," he admitted with an almost sinister smile. My stomach churned at the admission. Torture. He was torturing them.

"Why don't you just kill them," I asked, trying not to let the disgust I was feeling seep into my tone.

"Doctors may be able to learn surgery on a cadaver, but they will never understand medicine until they practice on living flesh," he offered the metaphor so calmly.

"What are you trying to find out?" I asked, seeing a sort of glint in his eye.

"Everything." Finishing his drink, he pushed off the counter and stood from his stool. He left a couple of bills on the bar and turned to face me.

"Three days, Archer. By this weekend, she will either need to join our ranks, or we will be forced to eliminate the threat."

I swallowed the lump in my throat and nodded. My eyes followed my father's imposing figure as he exited the bar, but even when he was gone, I couldn't seem to fill my lungs with air.

I let my head fall into my hands and sighed, feeling the tightness in my chest overwhelm me. How did I get here? How did I become… this?

I don't remember when I left the bar or when I arrived back at HQ. Everything happened in a slow haze. Suddenly, I was turning the door handle on my dad's office and stepping into the darkened room to see Athena, visibly paler and weaker than the last time I saw her. Her head lifted meekly, and her eyes met mine with an almost hopeless expression before slowly letting her head fall forward again.

"Athena," I said, stepping forward into the space. "You haven't been eating."

She didn't respond, remaining quiet and staring at the floor before her. I knelt in front of her, hoping she would make eye contact with me again.

"You need your strength," I whispered. She ignored me still. I didn't know when I made the choice or even why I made it in the first place, but I found myself desperately searching for answers that, at this crossroads, only she could offer. That fact was why I whispered the following words. "If I'm going to allow them to bite you, I need you to be strong enough to survive it."

Her head snapped up, and her eyes widened in surprise. Clearly, as shocked to hear what I had to say as I was to hear myself say it.

"You're going to let me see them?" She asked eagerly. Life was returning to her features with every passing moment.

"I don't.." I paused, realizing how dangerous this road was to travel. "I don't believe you yet. But I think if anyone seems so certain of something, they deserve a chance to prove it."

She smiled so brightly, so reminiscent of those easy afternoons at her bookstore, that I thought she might actually forgive me for this after all was said and done.

If she was still alive, that is.

"When?" She pleaded.

"Most everyone is gone for the night. We'll go now."

You'd think I had promised her a million dollars the way her face lit with hope.

"You're sure about this? I can't save you if they want to kill you, Athena."

She nodded eagerly.

"They won't hurt me. They're mine." There was a sort of apparent certainty and confidence in her tone that made me believe her. At least believe her enough to let her try.

"Come on, we have to hurry." I loosened her bindings and helped her stand from the chair. Her legs nearly gave out beneath her from lack of use over the past few days. I cursed under my breath quietly, feeling overwhelming guilt over her treatment, or rather lack thereof.

"Stay close to me, ok?" I commanded, and she nodded eagerly.

Glancing out the door into the hallway, I quickly led Athena through the silent passageways of the Nameless Head Quarters. I felt her holding her breath behind me, in either eager anticipation at seeing her vampires again or fear of running into someone she shouldn't out here in the hall.

By either a stroke of luck or fate itself, we made it to the door to the holding cells without being spotted. When we arrived at the iron doors, I swallowed the lump in my throat, remembering the last time I stood there.

"Archer." Her whispered voice brought me back to reality. "Are you ok?"

I couldn't help the guilt that crested in my chest at the fact that she was worried about me even though I was her captor.

"The last time I walked through these doors, a vampire nearly killed me," I stated, holding up my wrist for her. Her green eyes scanned the scar that was present there.

"How long were they held captive?" She asked an edge of judgment in her tone. My eyebrows rose in response.

"I don't know…" I admitted, hating the way her question had me rethinking everything I had known to be true.

"Captivity can change a person," she whispered, adverting her eyes from mine, but the words found their mark in my gut.

"I have to ask one last time, Athena," I started. "Are you sure about this?"

"Positive," she replied quickly, without hesitation.

With a deep sigh, I inserted the thick key into the door and pushed it open. The dark hallway was just as I remembered—eerie and desolate. It seemed to stretch on endlessly, each cell identical in its quiet desolation. Every step we took reverberated through the corridor, echoing the sound of solitude.

As we pressed forward, the darkness ahead seemed to grow even more oppressive. The long path continued, and with each step, we descended further into the heart of this chilling dungeon, toward The Wanderers, toward the memory of my worst experience.

"Stay behind the line," I offered, closing the door behind us and effectively locking us in. My heart rate picked up violently as I moved closer to the cell that used to hold Evangeline.

"Athena?" I heard a whispered and strained voice from down the hall call out.

Next to me, Athena nearly squealed with excitement at the sound of the vampire's voice. She began to jog forward, and I rushed to keep up with her. The moment we arrived in front of The Wanderer's cages, I felt my stomach pit deepen.

"Oh my god," she gasped.

The vamps exploded into a chorus of exclamations.

"Baby, you're here!"

"Oh, bookworm. I missed you."

"Darlin', you're ok!"

And the one from the diner, Orpheus, sighed deeply, letting his head fall forward in relief. A look of pure love and adoration painted on each of their faces. Athena began to rush toward them, but I gripped her shoulder to keep her from crossing the line into their outstretched arms.

The Wanderers released a collective growl.

"What the fuck is he doing here?" The tattooed one asked, staring at me with a murderous gaze.

"Baby, are you ok? Are you hurt?" Samara asked, her eyes scanned the woman at my side. Either she was a skilled performer, or the worry was genuine.

"I'm ok, I promise," Athena whispered. I turned to see a tear sliding down her cheek. I couldn't comprehend what I was seeing. True and honest emotion. I knew that Athena had claimed to love these creatures, but truthfully, I believed she was simply under some sort of spell, lost in their intoxication. But watching the relief on these vampires' faces proved that not only did she love them, but the feeling was mutual. I also couldn't help but notice that they were still relatively lively. Typically, after this many days of not feeding, the vampires in captivity start to show signs of decomposition and aggravation, but not The Wanderers.

Curious.

"How did you get out?" The shorter blonde one asked. Athena turned over her shoulder to glance at me.

"He's giving me a chance to prove to him that you're being set up."

I observed their reactions. Shock and mild confusion flashed across their faces. Orpheus narrowed his eyes at me.

"What do you mean, little nymph?" he asked.

"They have a file on you here, of all the people.." she paused. "Of all the people they think you've killed.

"Let me guess," the tattooed man began. "All little kids and puppy dogs, right?" His eyes flicked over her shoulder to rest on me. "Typical, Nameless scum."

"You're monsters who survive on the blood of innocent human beings," I spat at him, although I'd be lying if I didn't admit that the phrase did not feel as definite as it once had.

"That rhetoric certainly would make it easier for your kind to commit genocide," Orpheus seethed, his dark eyes blazing.

"You'd have to be alive for it to be considered that," I barked back.

"Please, stop," Athena interjected, looking between us. I broke the heated eye contact with Orpheus and turned my eyes to her. "I'm here to prove to you that they didn't do that, right?" I nodded curtly. "So please, let me."

I scanned the vampires before me. Their features were primarily human despite their slightly darkened red eyes. I expected a frenzy. I expected their hunger to take over, erasing the humanity from their disguises.

Although Evangeline was once just as composed. Until I got closer.

"This is a bad idea," I whispered, drawing a hand through my hair. "They're going to kill you, Athena."

Each vamp let out a growl at my statement.

"If you think we'd hurt one hair on our mate's head, then you are more idiotic than I first suspected," the tattooed behemoth said through bared teeth.

"Archer, they won't hurt me," Athena assured me, her tone filled with a kind of trust I'd never experienced myself.

"What is he talking about, bookworm? What are you going to prove?"

She stepped forward, but my grip remained on her shoulder. "I'm going to let one of you drink from me. Then close the wound."

I instantly felt the collective hunger rise in the room. But it wasn't the kind of hunger that told me she was in danger, but rather the type of hunger that told me she was coveted and desired.

I scanned their lust-filled expressions, and my confusion only grew.

"Will you let them all feed from me?" Athena asked, eagerly turning her gaze to me. I looked over at her, seeing her pale face and remembering her aversion to eating anything we had provided over the last few days.

"Even if they won't drain you dry, having four vamps feed from you would kill you in your condition." The moment the words were out of my mouth, the vamps hissed.

"What have you done to her?" Orpheus seethed.

"What condition?" Samara begged.

"She hasn't eaten in days," I began. "On her own volition," I added when their gazes turned murderous.

"The Hunter is right, little nymph. You wouldn't be strong enough for each of us to feed on you. And well…" he paused, shame filling his expression. "We're all pretty hungry right now." It was the first time they had mentioned their hunger, and honestly, now that they did mention it, they didn't seem like the rabid animals my father always made them out to be. I didn't know if it was part of some game to get us to lower our guard or if they genuinely weren't feeling the effects of their hunger. Either way, Orpheus didn't seem to want to take any chances with Athena's health.

"If you can't control yourself, then we shouldn't do this," I stated matter-of-factly.

The tattooed one gripped the bars of his enclosure and glared at me. "We can control ourselves just fine."

Orpheus cleared his throat softly, and the others seemed to take a step back.

"Only one," I responded, scanning their faces.

"As much as it pains me to say it, I agree with the Hunter," Orpheus bit back. Athena nodded, accepting that condition, but then she let her gaze fall to the floor and idly played with her fingers.

"I... I can't choose. I won't choose," she replied after a moment.

"We won't ever make you choose, Athena. Never," the blonde responded in a soft southern lilt.

"It needs to be the one of us who's most in control at the moment, just to be safe," Orpheus replied diplomatically. Athena nodded, accepting that.

"So, which one of you is it, then? Who's more in control of themselves?" I watched their faces momentarily as they attempted to determine the answer.

I hated the thought of leaving it to chance and letting them decide something so huge and vital so arbitrarily. I had made the choice before I even realized it, and suddenly, the flesh on my arm split beneath where I had pressed the blade of my knife into my skin.

A test, I told myself as I watched their reactions to the fresh, warm blood that poured down my arm onto the ground below.

Their eyes tracked it almost immediately. Reddening. They pressed forward in their cells, their features sharpening into the monsters I knew them to be. But just when I was prepared to fight back, to reach for the stake in my waistband and protect myself and Athena from their vicious natures, they surprised me.

Taking deep breaths, The Wanderers did something I didn't know a vampire was even capable of.

They controlled themselves.

Their features softened as they shook their heads and took calming, steadying breaths.

The shock must have been on my face as I tried to make sense of the information swirling in my mind. It was Orpheus who spoke first. "There is a lot you don't understand about us, Hunter." His red eyes seared into mine, and for the first time, I thought I believed him.

I looked back between him and Athena, who was staring at him, all of them, with such love and admiration in her gaze.

"Go ahead," I whispered, hating how the words felt on my lips. I was effectively betraying everything I've ever known. Every lesson that had been forcefully drilled into my head. Every time my father told me a horrific story or every time I attended a Hunter's funeral after these violent and unstable creatures mutilated them.

My hand instinctively gripped the handle of the wooden stake in my waistband as Athena rushed forward past the red line on the ground, and I braced myself for the tearing of flesh, the spilling of blood. Destruction. Death.

But it never came.

They didn't bite her. Instead, the moment she reached the first cage, she pushed her arms through the bars and embraced the creature within like they were her life source. The tattooed one held her back, breathing in her scent, but not once did his fangs penetrate her skin. Instead, he just soaked up the moment. When Athena repeated the process with each of the vamps, I watched in awe, unable to formulate any words. If it was all an act, it was one hell of a convincing one. She had tear-filled reunions with each of them, and with each passing second, years of hatred and fear began to slip away.

"Are you being treated well?" Orpheus asked tenderly as he flicked his eyes over to me briefly.

"Where they're holding me feels like a five-star hotel compared to these cells," she cried, tears slipping down her cheeks. "I've missed you all so much."

"We've missed you too, love," Samara added.

"I just found you. I can't lose you," Athena whispered, pain lacing every word. Her tears felt like barbed wire wrapping around my heart.

"We need to hurry," I choked out, hating how weak my voice sounded. I sounded broken. Like a man who just realized most of his beliefs have been wrong.

Athena wiped her wet eyes and nodded, turning back to her vamps. "I can't choose," she repeated.

I watched as Orpheus toiled over a decision in his mind. Eventually, he stepped forward, gripping Athena's hand through the bars and tenderly kissing the knuckles—an outpouring of emotion that I never expected from The Wanderers's vicious leader.

"Samara has the best self-control of all of us, and she'll be able to combat her hunger the easiest."

I waited to see if there would be some sort of argument or fight, but they all seemed to agree with Orpheus' assessment. They shared her love, affection, and blood so seamlessly, without a hint of reservation or jealousy. It was a strangely beautiful thing to witness.

Athena nodded, kissing Orpheus' hand where he held her before turning and stopping before Samara's cell. The vamp's eyes were full of intensity and heat. So much so that if I hadn't needed to witness the bite, I would have preferred to turn around and give them privacy.

Athena approached Samara slowly, their gazes locked together. When Samara reached out a hand through the cage and caressed Athena's cheek, pushing a strand of red hair behind her ear, I could feel the love bursting in the air.

"I will never hurt you," Samara whispered, bringing Athena's arm to her lips and planting a kiss on the inside of her wrist.

Athena let a small gasp out at the contact and nodded. "I know."

Then Samara sunk her fangs into the flesh of Athena's arm. My own scar burned with the phantom memory of the pain, and Evangeline's red, empty eyes flashed in my mind. I waited for Athena to call out in agony or to beg for my help. But instead, she let out the softest moan and caressed Samara's face as she drank. That alone would have been enough to shock me, but then Samara did something unbelievable.

She pulled away.

Her lips were painted red with Athena's blood, and her features had sharpened, but there was a humanity in her red eyes that there never was with Evangeline.

I found myself stepping forward, my eyes trained on the dark red wound on Athena's wrist that was obscured by flowing blood. Like a moth to the flame, I approached. Without letting Athena go, Samara let her tongue dance across the wound, a step that I was entirely unfamiliar with. We Hunters never stuck around long enough for a vamp to try something like that with us.

Samara pressed a kiss into Athena's palm, then placed her cheek there. Closing her eyes, she sighed, relishing in the physical contact.

When Athena pulled her hand back, she turned to find me hovering just behind her. She held out her arm for me, and I watched as the skin around the wound began healing. Slowly, nearly unnoticeable, but within a few minutes, Athena's pale skin was unblemished.

As if nothing happened.

I stumbled backward, my breath rushing out in ragged spurts.

"Archer, you see the truth now, don't you?"

I shook my head—not in disagreement, but in disbelief, in hurt. This truth could not exist simultaneously with all the truths I've ever known, and no matter how prepared I was to test the theory, I never considered this outcome.

"We need to get you back to the office," I muttered, unable to make eye contact with her.

"Archer, please," she pleaded.

"Athena, we're going to get out of here. I swear to you," Orpheus claimed, not even bothering to whisper in my presence. Maybe he saw just how broken I'd become and no longer saw me as a threat. Was I a threat? Could I be if I needed to be? I wasn't so sure anymore.

"We'll see you soon," the blonde promised lovingly.

"You're my soul, bookworm," the tattooed one pledged.

I needed to process new information, but until then, I had one last question to answer.

"Athena, please. We need to go now. I.. I need a minute to think about this," I begged.

She glanced at each of her vamps, placing a hand on her heart and nodding solemnly. "Ok. I'll go with you."

She stopped by my side and waited for me to lead her out. As we began our walk down the hall away from The Wanderers, I heard one of them call out.

"If she is harmed in any way, I will personally hold you responsible," Orpheus warned. I didn't turn to look at him. Instead, I quickly rushed Athena back through the iron doors at the end of the hall. She followed me silently, trusting me to guide her safely through the hallways back to the office.

She even allowed me to replace her bindings when we arrived. She was calm. Content.

"How are you so calm right now?" I asked incredulously. She sighed deeply before meeting my eyes.

"You let me see them," she claimed, a single tear sliding down her cheek. "I needed to see them."

My eyes trained on my father's desk— a sturdy wood behemoth, just as intimidating now as it was all those years ago. He never let me in here unaccompanied while I was growing up. He was rarely not occupying that leather chair, but now that his room had become a pseudo-holding cell, it meant that he had vacated the space for the time being. Leaving his things open and unguarded.

My feet carried me behind the desk before I could even stop them. I felt Athena's eyes on me, and I ignored the way they burned into my skin. The top drawer was relatively standard. Office supplies, post-its, pens, paperclips. It was strange thinking that a Vampire Hunter still had use for such mundane supplies.

The next drawer was a little more detailed. Files on different vampire sightings and the personnel files on each of the cadets from this year's class. So many names of people being indoctrinated into this life the same way I was. The brand burned slightly as I scanned the files.

Three more drawers and I hadn't found anything that might explain this new development. All the while, Athena remained silent, just watching me. I almost gave up. I wasn't even sure what I thought I was going to find. Just something. Anything that could help me make sense of this jumbled mess in my mind.

Then I saw the latch.

Small, silver, hidden. Sucking in a deep breath of air, I pressed down. When a metallic release rang out, I could hear my blood running through my veins, echoing in the silent room.

The small compartment beneath the final drawer hung open, waiting for me to dive into the answers it held. I hesitated. I couldn't help it. Everything was changing, and something in my gut told me that the contents of this hidden compartment would ruin me. I sat crouched behind my father's desk, thankful that Athena's eyes couldn't reach me from where I was.

My hand slipped into the darkness and wrapped around the hilt of a metallic weapon. My heart pumped wildly, viciously, uncontrollably. Everything was leading up to this moment—my whole life, my training, meeting Athena, capturing The Wanderers, defying my father.

The weapon looked like a dagger, but instead of one long blade, there were two thin, pointed prongs in its place. It was like a thicker, more violent version of those skewers I used to roast marshmallows with, but something told me that this weapon was not used for such frivolity.

I rolled up my sleeve and slowly pressed the tips of the blades against my skin, where I had punctured it down in the cells. It stung, and I winced in pain. The hollow hilt warmed to the touch and whirred to life. Suddenly, the small blade emanated a soft glow, and as if it were being vacuumed, my blood was drawn by the device, drained from my vein, and pooled into the hilt. I cried out and pulled the blade from my skin, stopping the painful process before it could do anything else. As the blade was lifted from my skin, there they were. Two perfect puncture wounds. It was not unlike all the photos I had shown Athena, albeit it was much shallower. Every photo. Every single one.

My head was spinning, and my heart thumped in my chest as I stared at my blood that now sat in a thin layer within the hollow hilt.

Shock. Grief. Anger. Betrayal.

There was no chance of me sorting through my emotions at that moment, but one thing was sure. I needed to get out of this room as soon as possible. Without bothering to clean the blade, I threw it back into the compartment and closed it. Standing from my crouched position, I ambled toward Athena, who simply watched me.

There were a million things I wanted to say, but I couldn't find a single word worthy of the current state of my thoughts.

I glanced over at the day-old food that sat untouched on my father's desk.

"I'll get new food sent up for you." I began to leave, but I heard her call out my name. I paused, unwilling to turn to see her, tied to that chair by my hand.

"You know, don't you? You know that they didn't do this. Please, tell me you see it."

I swallowed the lump in my throat and fought the sting in my eyes.

"I have to go," I mumbled before rushing out of the office door and locking it behind me. I couldn't catch a full breath if I wanted to.

And I'm not so sure I wanted to.

LAZ

EIGHT

On the morning of our twelfth day in captivity, Bennett decided to see how Vampires reacted to being doused in holy water. He started with Silas. It was a clever tactic. Honestly, I had to hand it to him. Silas was the most physically strong of the four of us, so when his screams echoed through the cages, it was a clear indication that we were in for some pain. If even the strongest among us couldn't handle the torture, we stood no chance. He took Samara next, and in true Samara fashion, she managed to hold in her screams for a while, but even her iron will eventually stood no chance against the burning liquid. I wondered how much of her longer resistance had to do with the blood of our mate that flowed through her body. I knew Orpheus' plan was for us to convince Bennett that we were in much worse shape than we truly were, but something about her screams and the way Silas was still shivering in pain in his cage told me there wasn't a whole lot of pretending going on.

Because Bennett and Orpheus had some strange 'macho stand-off' energy between them, and his idea of torture for our leader is to make him wait for his turn and listen to the pained screams of his coven, I was next.

In another horrific display of their torturous renovation of these cells, three small sprinkler heads lowered from the ceiling, and a moment later, the evil little spouts were showering me with liquid death. It sliced against my back as I crumbled to my knees with a scream trapped in my throat. The physical pain had always been something that didn't affect me as hard as the emotional and mental anguish I had faced in my life, but damn, first the sun, then the holy water. It was enough to make me reconsider.

I pushed all thoughts from my head as I let the water wash over me, drenching my clothing and clinging to every inch of my skin. It burnt the way acid might affect a human. It was vicious and violent. A perfect cocktail. Three parts holy water and one part garlic. Nice touch, I thought as I analyzed the makeup of the liquid. It hurt. Unimaginably. I let my mind focus on her, my mate. Her soft red curls, her stunning green eyes, the way her lips part slightly when she's experiencing pleasure. Her image, so clearly burned into my mind, was the one thing that could soften the sting of the water against my skin. I focused on the chemical mixture. I felt its contents as it poured onto my skin. Despite the strength she gave me, I still felt the fierce sting pelt against me. Fuck, I'd give anything for this to be nice soothing water right about now.

The mixture continued its persistent assault on my skin, but with each passing second, the sting subsided until the liquid running down my skin felt almost…relieving?

I focused on it. I felt the chemical makeup of it in my mind. It couldn't be true. But it was.

It was water.

I glanced at Bennett out of the corner of my eye, expecting him to make some comment about it, but he didn't. Instead, he watched with evil intensity as his torture continued.

Had I done that? Had I changed the chemical makeup of his holy water acid? I'd never been able to do such a thing before. I covered the smile that played on my lips with my fingers and sent a warming embrace down the bond to my mate. The woman whose love made me powerful. The woman who made me a better version of myself.

Stay strong, Laz.

I heard her voice echo in my head.

Athena, darlin', is that you?

I called back through the channels of my mind.

It's me. I'm here! You can hear me!

I nearly smiled, but I knew that Bennett was watching closely, so I hid the movement of my lips with a snarl before calling back to her through the channels of my mind.

I can hear you.

I felt her joy push through the bond.

I feel your fear, Laz. It's ok. We will get through this. Together.

I felt my heart nearly burst from the adoration I held for her as I responded.

I know we will.

The mental connection faltered, then slipped away, but her strength remained.

With her in my heart, I could withstand any pain.

But Bennett couldn't know that.

So, I fell to my knees and screamed out in agony, maybe a little over the top, but hey, it wasn't often that I was given the opportunity to put on a little show. When the water stopped, relief flooded my body. I felt Samara's healing touch graze my back, working at undoing the damage the water had done before my gift worked its magic, but I didn't dare let that relief show. Instead, I held my knees to my chest and heaved long and labored breaths. I heard Samara and Silas doing the same. The Hunters would be letting their guard down any day now. They have been torturing us and withholding blood from us. They will be expecting us to be weak. The truth is, at this moment, I've never felt stronger.

Bennett whispered some overt taunt to Orpheus before turning on the spouts in his cell. I heard Orpheus let out a grunt of pain as the mixture landed on his skin. I closed my eyes tightly, focusing on the rushing water's sound, feeling how it hit the ground and spread across the concrete floor. I willed for the harmful chemicals within the water to dissipate, begging my mind and my power to remove anything that could hurt him.

I couldn't tell right away if it had worked. Sounds of agony echoed from Orpheus' cell, and it was so convincing that I couldn't tell if it was real or his attempt at convincing Bennett. But when I focused on the liquid again, it had run clear. The water was pure and harmless.

I heard Bennett take cautious steps toward Orpheus' cell when the rushing water subsided.

"Why are you doing this?" Orpheus pleaded, and I couldn't contain the smile on my face. I let my chin fall to the floor so nobody could see the joy on my face. There isn't a universe where Orpheus would beg like that. He was pretending. Which meant we were winning.

"Our world would be better off without your kind," Bennett spat back. I rolled my eyes. 'Blah blah blah, racist shit.' That's all he ever said, like a broken record of unyielding hatred. I couldn't wait to kill him. Bigots really got me riled up.

"Why won't you just kill us?" Orpheus cried out. Oh, he was good. Let the Hunter see weakness and get him to show his hand.

Bennett chuckled darkly, a great sign that an evil villain monologue was about to occur. "I'll kill you when I'm good and ready," he responded.

"You're a monster," Orpheus seethed.

"Oh, I'm the monster? That's rich, coming from you lot," he was becoming unhinged— exactly where we needed him. "Always hiding in the shadows. Preying on the helpless. You monsters aren't worthy of the gifts you receive."

Bingo.

"We didn't ask for these gifts," Orpheus whispered, playing directly into his hand.

"Well, soon enough, you won't have to worry about those anymore." Bennett stepped away, letting his murderous gaze wash over each of us before he headed down the long corridor and disappeared behind the metallic door.

Standing, I attempted to wipe the excess liquid from my clothing as Samara spoke.

"What happened, Orpheus?" She sounded almost frantic. "When I went to heal you, I didn't feel any injury." I smiled brightly.

"I'm not sure," he responded.

"You can thank me for that," I called out softly, making my way to the bars of my cage and leaning my arms on the cool metal.

"What do you mean?" Silas asked, grunting as he stood to his feet.

"I guess it's my fun little upgrade courtesy of our mate," I beamed, feeling so proud of my bond with my beautiful Athena.

"You could manipulate the contents of the water?" Orpheus whispered as a question, but his incredulous tone told me he already knew the answer.

"What the hell, why didn't you stop mine? Hurt like a fucking bitch," Silas griped.

"I didn't realize I could until it happened to me," I called back.

"So far, all of us, save for Silas, have received some sort of power upgrade," Orpheus began.

"You still haven't told us what your fancy new skill is, Orpheus," Silas teased. "And I already have the coolest power ever, no upgrade needed, thank you very much."

I chuckled at that, and the others joined in with soft, gleeful laughter. As our laughs settled, I sighed deeply.

"We have been here for over a week and were just tortured, and yet here we are…laughing," I whisper. The others release their own content sighs. We all knew the reason for our strengthened resolve this time around. It was her.

"When we make our move, we're going to need to kill them all." It was Silas who first broke the silence. "We all agree on that, right?"

I nodded but didn't voice the words. It was the only logical choice, but that didn't mean it was any less daunting. Even with our strength intact, they outnumbered us at least ten to one. They were intimately aware of our weaknesses and were trained on how to exploit them. It's the reason they were such a formidable opponent. The reason that so many of our kind have been eradicated. That is why we were among the few covens left, as far as we know.

"It's been almost two weeks. When are we doing this, Orpheus?" Samara asked, an eagerness to her tone.

I heard him take a deep breath and walk a few paces within his cell. I imagined him wringing out the water from his clothes and running a hand through his tangled mop of hair.

"They're after our gifts. Bennet and his useless big mouth just made that abundantly clear. As far as we know, they are only aware of yours, Silas. From the last escape."

I shuddered as the memory of that night came into focus.

"We can't let them discover what we can do, especially not now that our powers have grown. If they put it together if they find out why we're stronger now…" He didn't have to finish that thought. We knew. If the Hunters knew that Athena's bond to us was what made us stronger, they would either try to turn her to see what sort of amplification happened when we were all vampires. Or… they'd eliminate the bond and weaken us.

I refused to let either of those things happen.

Not like this.

"So tomorrow?" Silas prompted.

There was an anxious silence that filled the cells then. Despite the newfound upgrades and the game we had been playing, we still had to perform the Herculean task of escaping the Hunter's facility for a second time. And I knew I wasn't the only one thinking about how not all of us made it out last time around.

Five in, four out.

And that was when all of us were vampires, strong, fast, and powerful. This time, we had a human to protect. This time, there were five in… and we were going to do everything in our power to get five out. No matter the cost.

"Tomorrow," Orpheus responded. "We make our move tomorrow."

ATHENA

NINE

After finishing my count of the ceiling and floor tiles in this room for the seventh time, I released a long and pain-filled sigh. It had been a few days since I saw my Wanderers, and I was getting restless. I felt their absence so profoundly, so viciously, but another sharp pain was snaking its way through my soul. Just the thought of what my absence was doing to my grandma was enough to wrench a sob from my chest. She's been through too much lost too many people. I wish I could tell her I was alive. That I was ok. That I was coming home.

After Mom passed, Grandma was the one who remained strong while I fell apart at the seams. Her gentle strength was steadfast and comforting. To anyone, it seemed she was handling the loss incredibly well. But I knew her better than that. She was broken. Her soul had splintered, and in the absence of two pieces of her heart, she was lost. She refused to show that to anyone, though. I pressed my eyes tight, trying to picture her face, latching onto her memory in search of that same comfort.

"Are you ready, Athena? Guests are arriving." My grandma called from the base of

the stairs. I was jolted from my thoughts. My feet had brought me down the hall toward my mother's room. As I looked into the space from the safety of the threshold, the air felt heavy with grief and the remnants of happy and horrific memories. The sunlight filtered through the soft white and blue curtains, casting a muted glow on the familiar surroundings that had once been filled with the warmth of my mother's soul. Everything seemed frozen in time as if the world outside had moved on while this room remained suspended in a bittersweet moment. This room hadn't been hers in a while, not since she stopped being able to make the trip up the stairs.

The bed was neatly made with the light purple comforter we'd picked out together. The floral pattern on the bedspread, once a comforting sight, now felt like a distant echo of happier days. A photograph on the bedside table of the time when Mom, Grandma, Grandpa, and I went to the Zoo. Those frozen smiles seemed to mock the somber reality of the world I found myself in now. Half of those smiles were gone now.

"Almost," I called back, trying to turn my head away from the site before me but finding myself unable to tear my eyes from the ghosts of the past. My feet moved on their own, taking step after cautious step into her space.

The silence was palpable, broken only by the occasional creak of the floorboards beneath my tentative feet. The room echoed with memories. Each piece of furniture held a story of its own. The dresser we painted together in the backyard. The purple plush loveseat we saw on the side of the road that she fell in love with and begged me to help carry the three blocks home in the rain. The books on the shelf she would read to me when I couldn't sleep, and the books she swore she would read one day but never got the chance to. The bed where I would crawl beneath the covers in the middle of the night when I couldn't sleep and I felt like the monsters under the bed would get me. She'd brush my hair out of my eyes and hold me tight, promising me that monsters didn't exist.

I heard a soft murmur of conversation drifting up from the stairs, reminding me of the world outside — a world that continued to move forward.

Summoning the strength to leave the room, I took a deep breath and steadied myself, breathing in the lingering scent of her perfume. How long until that scent dissipates?

When you lose someone, you lose them a million little times. Over and over and over again. I will lose her the first time I watch a sunset without her. The first time I hear her favorite song. The first time I take a deep breath in this room and, her scent doesn't greet me. The first time I find the love of my life and she isn't there to walk me down the aisle. I have a harrowing feeling that I'd be losing my mom for the rest of my life—a little bit more each and every day.

The hallway felt endless as I made my way toward the staircase. As I descended, the murmur of voices grew louder. The somber atmosphere of the wake encircled me before I even reached the bottom landing.

As I entered the living room, the sting in my eyes intensified as I watched friends and family huddle together, sharing stories and offering condolences. Mom would have loved to have everyone she cared about in one room like this. All the business owners from the pier, Davia, her family, our neighbors, and the community members who knew and loved her. They were all here. There, at the heart of it all, stood my grandmother. She smiled a soft sort of grin that was a beacon of resilience.

Though clouded with the same grief that we all shared, her eyes bore a quiet strength that perplexed me. She had weathered her own storms, lost her own battles, and emerged on the other side, and still managed to smile. I couldn't fathom the sort of strength required for that kind of feat. Grandma noticed me standing at the base of the stairs, and with a gentle nod, she beckoned me to her side. In that simple gesture, she conveyed a silent understanding that needed no words. As I approached, she enveloped me in a tender embrace, her arms a source of comfort in the midst of sorrow.

With a soft squeeze, Grandma guided me to join the crowd of people gathered. She spoke of fond memories, shared anecdotes that celebrated my mother's life, and expertly navigated the delicate line between grief and remembrance.

Amid my mother's wake, surrounded by tearful eyes and heavy hearts, I couldn't help but marvel at her strength. In that moment, as we faced the collective ache of saying goodbye to my mother and all the memories we had shared, I found solace in the last remaining member of my family.

Tears fell down my cheeks and landed on my lap as I let myself wallow in the misery of knowing what my absence was doing to her. To them all. Another constricting sob spilled from my throat as I considered Davia. Would I ever see them again? Would I ever see the shop again? Even if I somehow escaped this, would I ever be able to return home? If I had to choose between my mates and my family… I couldn't do it. Even the thought of being forced to decide had my stomach turning over painfully.

The door handle turned, and I willed the tears to slow, composing myself as best I could. I didn't want Archer to see me at my weakest. My body tensed as I braced for the confrontation. My shoulders were screaming at the pain of being bound behind my back for so long. I was sure they would be permanently damaged if it weren't for Samara's gentle touch that came to me each night to ease the continuous ache. Footsteps inside were followed by the door closing once again. He hadn't said anything yet, so I kept my head down.

He waited by the door for a moment before turning to head for the desk. It wasn't until he had taken a few steps that a dangerous realization came to me. That wasn't how Archer walked. The gait was off, and the pattern was more assured. Archer walked around me as if he felt like I could break with one wrong move. No, these steps were confident, strong, and heavy. I lifted my head just enough to peer up at the figure through the curtain of my lashes and unkempt hair that had fallen into my face.

His broad shoulders were draped in a well-tailored black suit. His dark, auburn hair was neatly combed away from his face. He had a prominent brow bone and a sharp jaw that carried the slightest echo of a 5 o'clock shadow. I had never seen this man before, and yet something about him seemed familiar. He didn't turn to look at me but ruffled through some of the things on the desk. What was he looking for? I diverted my eyes from him as his shoulders squared to face me.

"You must be wondering who I am."

I was, but I didn't let him know that.

"I don't think it's in our best interests to share personal details just yet." His voice was grave, like he had lost his voice recently, and his timbre was still a result of that. "So you can call me J."

I didn't respond, and I didn't raise my eyes to meet his. He slowly made his way around the desk toward me. Instinctually, I shied away from his advances. He stopped just a few feet short and leaned back on his desk, crossing his legs at the ankle and folding his arms across his chest. I couldn't tell without looking at him, but it seemed like my reaction amused him. Perhaps fear was a response he expected from his prisoners, and I was delivering.

"This is my office that you've been holed up in. Can't say I'm too happy about the stench."

I cringed. Truthfully, I'd gotten a little nose blind to myself. Archer and the other door guard brought me food. When Archer couldn't be bothered to show his face, both let me use the restroom when needed, but I still hadn't taken a shower.

They offered to let me take one a few days ago, but the idea of being naked in this place, being vulnerable with all these men around me, thinking I'm their prisoner? Not a chance. If my *stench* kept them from placing their hands on me, then I would wear it proudly.

"I'm sure Archer told you why you've been here for so long," he prompted, but again I stayed quiet. If you let someone talk long enough, they are bound to give away their secrets. "Chatty little girl, aren't you?" He grumbled frustratedly.

He unfolded his arms to grab the desk on either side of his hips that rested on the edge. His fingertips rapped against the wood for a few painfully quiet moments. Finally, he sighed and pushed off the desk to step forward. I forced my body not to react. I refused to give this man an ounce of the fear he so clearly craved.

"Maybe I can see why my son has been wasting all this time getting you to cooperate," he whispered under his breath. Son? I tried to picture Archer with a similar hair shade, and it was so clear. Of course. That's why he seemed so familiar. I'd seen those features in my captor.

"I do not cooperate with kidnappers," I stated with as steady a voice as I could muster. He seemed pleased that I had finally responded.

"Clearly." He then moved to another side of the room, opposite the big desk. He opened a cabinet I had found myself staring at on more than one occasion and grabbed a glass container with a dark amber liquid swirling inside. He poured a shot into an empty glass and replaced the carafe. All the while, I watched his back. He was strong and confident. He was playing a mind game with me, and I wouldn't let him.

"So, J, are you here to tell me I get to go home now?" I asked, trying to craft a facade of bravado for the intimidating figure in front of me. He turned again, and I kept my eyes hidden behind my hair but watched him with rapt attention. Each move he made was deliberate, like a well-choreographed dance—perfectly designed to intimidate and scare me.

"Give me a reason why I should," he asked casually as if he was considering accepting my business proposal and not deciding the fate of my freedom.

"I'm not a threat to you." It was the truth. I wanted no part of whatever was happening here. I wanted to leave this place with my mates and never return or think about this time of our lives again.

"It does not take physical strength to be a threat to me," he started, taking a long drink from his glass. "That is a guarded secret, something I work very hard to ensure my enemies never learn."

"I'm not your enemy."

"But you know who my enemy is. And my son tells me you've become very comfortable with them."

I swallowed deeply. How much did Archer tell him?

"Did your son also tell you that The Wanderers are being framed for everything you think they've done?"

This caught him off guard. For the first time since he walked through the door, there was a moment when the perfectly designed exterior cracked. It was gone before I could even register that it had happened, but I had thrown him off.

I could do it again.

"So, you do know what they are and what they've done," he mused once he had composed himself.

"Allegedly," I replied. He choked out a soft laugh.

"Were the graphic photos in this file still not enough to convince you?" He accused, his hands sliding through the discarded files on his desk.

"They didn't do that," I spat.

"You don't know what you're talking about, little girl."

"I'm not a fucking 'little girl' so stop calling me that!" I barked. He held his hands up in feigned surrender and chuckled.

"What's your name?" He asked.

"Thought we weren't sharing personal details," I tossed back, lacing my tone with as much indignation as possible.

"Let me tell you how this is going to go, little girl," he seethed, spitting those words with so much venom I almost felt my chest go numb as they found purchase. "You're either going to tell me what you know about The Wanderers, or you're going to die."

"I don't really like those options," I whispered, buying some time to think.

"Too fucking bad, you're forgetting who has all the power here."

"Hard to remember when I have no idea who you are. As far as I know, Archer is the one in charge here."

He rushed forward, another crack in the facade. I braced myself for his attack, but he stopped himself just before his hand made contact with my cheek.

"You're trying to rile me up," he said with pride like he had just deduced something impossible.

"It's working," I replied, lowering my chin to hide the smirk on my lips.

I could practically hear his teeth grinding from here.

"You want to defend those monsters down there, huh? What makes you think they didn't do what they're accused of?"

I could tell him the same thing I told Archer about the closing of the wounds, but something about the way his breathing was becoming ragged told me this man before me only had so much restraint left, and fuck, for some reason, I didn't want him to hurt Archer. I have no idea why I cared what happened to that traitor, but damnit. I did.

"Because I know them, they wouldn't do that."

His laugh had ice running through my veins.

"Oh, I see what's going on here. Did you whore yourself out to them? Is that it? Are you their fucking blood bag?"

My blood boiled.

"Do not call me that."

"Ah, I've hit a nerve then. You'll sleep with blood-sucking murderers, but you'll draw the line at being called a whore? How self-righteous of you."

"If anyone is a murderer here, it's you."

The composure he had held such a tight grip on had snapped, and he pressed forward, leaning down into my space. His hand grabbed at my chin and forcefully pulled it up so that I was forced to make unhindered eye contact with him for the first time. His emerald eyes burned with anger, and his lips were pulled back in a snarl. His hand on my skin sent a shockwave of panic through my body, and I couldn't control the fear then. What was he going to do to me? Could I stop him?

As I began spiraling, I saw his eyebrows furrow as he took in my face. His unfamiliar gaze held me captive as a shadow of an emotion passed across his hardened face.

"What is your name?" He asked again, his tone more inquisitive than angry this time.

When I didn't answer, choosing instead to suck in lungfuls of cool air to stave off the panic attack that threatened to claim me, he pulled back, dropping my chin and taking deliberate steps backward.

As he left, a strange look twisted his features, a mix of confusion and something more profound – a vulnerability that contradicted the menacing aura he exuded. His eyes once filled with a cold intensity, now held a hint of turmoil, as if an unexpected revelation had shaken him to the core. I strained against my restraints, watching with a mix of fear and curiosity as he cast one last glance back at me. There was a momentary hesitation in his step, a pause that betrayed an internal struggle. It was as if the walls he had meticulously built around himself were crumbling, revealing a vulnerability he hadn't anticipated.

When he left, closing the door behind him and leaving me alone in darkness once again, I didn't feel the similar sense of dread and fear close in around me. Whoever he was, he was affected by what I had said, by what he saw in here. For just a moment, I felt like maybe, just maybe, we could win.

ARCHER

TEN

The dull thud of my wrapped hands meeting the heavy bag echoed through the dimly lit gym. Beads of sweat trickled down my forehead as I unleashed a barrage of punches, each strike a desperate attempt to drown out the nagging doubts that had taken residence in my mind.

The rhythmic sound of flesh meeting fabric became my makeshift therapy. With its cold metallic scent and flickering fluorescent lights, the gym was a refuge where I could grapple with the guilt and confusion that clung to me like a heavy shadow. The pain against my knuckles was the last thing keeping me grounded. With each jab, I tried to silence the voices questioning my cause's validity. Was I fighting for the right side, or was I mindlessly following a path that had been hand-crafted by my father to promote death and destruction? The bag absorbed my uncertainty as I let the turmoil loose in each punch.

As I threw hooks and crosses, I couldn't shake the image of the kind-hearted redhead being held hostage in the office just a floor beneath my feet. Her words lingered in my mind like a haunting melody, a discordant reminder that taunted the possibility that she held a truth I was unwilling to acknowledge. The guilt gnawed at me, threatening to unravel the very fabric of my convictions.

The heavy bag swung in response to my blows, an unwitting partner in this internal battle. As I threw myself into the workout, I couldn't stop the onslaught of worry that maybe my father and this cause I was fighting for was, in fact, wrong.

My father's convictions were so strong, so steadfast, I had unquestioningly believed them. I considered them the indisputable truth, but Athena's convictions are just as strong. She was just as convinced that her Wanderers were the victims here as my father was convinced they were the monsters. How do you uncover the truth when both sides believe they're on the right side of history? Flashes of facts, memories, and conflicting truths that I had been force-fed flooded my mind with each punch of the bag.

Evangaline had bitten me. She was going to kill me.

She was being held captive and tortured.

The Wanderers killed that missing guy.

He tried to hurt Athena.

My father had some strange device that leaves behind vampire bites.

Vampire bites can close.

The Wanderers didn't kill Athena when they had the chance.

My father wouldn't do the same....

Breathing heavily, I finally relented, letting my battered hands fall to my side as I stepped away from the heavy bag. The gym's air felt thick with the residue of my internal struggle. With a sense of purpose, or perhaps desperation, I approached the gym's exit.

As I descended the stairs, the weight of all this uncertainty closed in on me, making me feel claustrophobic. I had made a choice, one that would have me walking a tightrope between loyalty and doubt. I would listen to her. She deserved to tell her side of this story, and I needed to hear it.

I'd listen to her and come to my own conclusions. Then, I would make the choice that had been looming over me for the last two weeks.

The corridor was empty, except for the owner of a muffled voice coming from around the corner near Athena's room. As I approached, I lightened my steps and listened as the familiar voice became clearer.

"Listen, I just wanted to check in." My father's voice sounded calm on the outside, and to anyone else, the demeanor would be believable, but I knew his tells and could hear the slight hitch and the way his voice pitched up. He was nervous. Shaken. I hugged the wall and carefully listened, straining to hear the voice on the other end of the conversation.

A muffled sound echoed from a phone speaker. It was too quiet to make out any words, but the feminine voice seemed frantic.

"Wait, slow down," he urged. Another few moments of quiet as he listened to the response. "Yes, we got them. I told you we would. But that's not why I'm calling. How is Athena?"

I furrowed my brow. Was this his mysterious contact? The one who told him we would find The Wanderers in Shockgrove. Why was he asking them about Athena?

"How long?" He followed up, a tenseness in his tone that I'm not sure I've heard since the day I crossed the red line. The voice responded, and I heard my father groan a pain-filled, angry sound.

"Why the fuck didn't you call me?" he hissed. The voice on the phone raised, and I knew my father was getting an earful for the tone he just used. "Right, no, I know... I was busy. Fuck." He groaned as the memory of Carmen's name appearing on his phone at the bar returned to me. "You should have tried harder to reach me," he accused. "Because I'm pissed off, Carmen. I'm her fucking father. I should have known she was missing."

My blood ran cold, and my lungs weren't capable of taking a breath. My father's cryptic conversation suddenly made chilling sense, and the weight of his words settled over me with a suffocating intensity. As the words reverberated in my mind, a nauseating realization dawned. Our hostage, the woman I'd kidnapped, the woman who I betrayed, was not merely a stranger caught in a dangerous battle with the monsters of the night....

She was my sister.

The world around me seemed to warp. The walls felt like they were closing in as I grappled with the enormity of this revelation.

"I'll fix this," my father spat before hanging up the phone. I slid down onto the floor, my legs unable to hold the weight of both me and this new secret. My father's breaths came in rapid spurts. I'd never witnessed him having a panic attack, but if he did, I'd assume it would sound something like this.

"Fuck!" He yelled, and a crashing sound came not long after. His phone exploded into pieces as the tech splintered against the wall and slid across the ground. He stormed off in the opposite direction, luckily for me, because I was not sure I could move from this spot if the building came crumbling down around me.

I don't know how long I sat there, flipping through my childhood memories, combing through each one, and looking for a clue, some indication that my father had this monumental secret. There was nothing—nothing I could think of that might have pointed to this entire other family that my father left behind.

Athena told me how old she was during one of our conversations, and I was less than a year younger. At the time, she teased me about it almost like a sibling would. What happened in that short time to force my father away from her and into his new family?

I felt sick to my stomach, and the walls around me were spinning. His lies had kept my sister from me. What else could he be lying about?

There wasn't guilt in my chest anymore. At least not the kind that worried me about questioning my father and everything he'd taught me. Our entire relationship was a lie. My whole life was a lie. When I stood from my seat on the floor and braced myself on the wall, I felt determination. Clarity.

The walk to her room was short, but it may as well have been miles. By the time I approached her door, I had made the choice that just an hour ago weighed so heavily on my chest and felt impossible.

When the door opened, she raised her eyes to meet mine, and something I can only describe as regret and love overtook my senses. How could I have possibly missed it? The more I looked at her, the more the intricate tapestry of our shared lineage unfolded. The red hair, the green eyes — they were markers of a hidden connection that now bound us together. She was my sister, undeniably.

She looked relieved to see me. Something I felt entirely too unworthy of. Her eyes searched mine with a mix of surprise and hope. The air between us crackled with unspoken words, the weight of our shared history hanging like an invisible thread.

"Are you okay?" I asked, my voice a low murmur.

She nodded, the confusion evident in her eyes. "I wasn't sure you were going to come back."

I stepped toward her, determined and resolute. She didn't shy away but instead watched me with rapt attention as I crossed behind her and cut through the bindings at her wrists, freeing her.

She said nothing, but I felt her questioning gaze burn into my skin.

I held out a hand, and she took it tentatively, rising from the confines of her captivity. The room seemed to expand as we stood there, siblings who were now united by a shared determination to unravel the truth. But she couldn't know that. I wouldn't be responsible for telling her who had done this to her. She had already lost so much in her life. I couldn't be the one to give her a father only for him to be a monster.

"What are you doing?" She whispered, fear lacing her tone. She didn't trust me. I deserved that, but damn if it didn't hurt to know that my actions had caused my sister harm. It was the fear in her gaze and the nerves in her voice that spurred me forward. There wasn't a doubt in my mind any longer. The choice had been made.

"I'm going to get you out of here, Athena. I'm setting you free."

ORPHEUS

ELEVEN

It was well into the evening when her emotions slammed into me. Since we completed the mate bond, I have been able to feel her more intensely. Honestly, I'd been able to feel everything more intensely. But her emotions felt different this time than they had these last few days. It wasn't fear that she was feeling panic or anger; instead, I felt relief and hope flood her. It was a euphoric rush of positive emotions that I hadn't felt from her since we last saw her. Something had made her happy…hopeful. I hated not being able to form that mental connection with her that both Samara and Laz had, but that fact didn't make me jealous as it may have at one point in time. Instead, I was thankful that at least one of us had been able to connect with her so she didn't feel so alone.

Leaning forward against the cool bars of the cage, I focused on her and the hope radiating from her emotions. Despite being a dangerous energy to feel in a place like this, it warmed my chest. I couldn't help but wonder what had her risking disappointment to feel it now.

"Laz, Samara, have either of you spoken to Athena tonight?" I whispered, knowing my coven had heard me just fine. Despite being trapped for two weeks, our strength remained relatively intact. Thanks to our mate. We would need blood soon, but we weren't withering away like we had been at this point of our last capture.

"Not yet," Samara offered.

"No, I tried earlier but couldn't get through," Laz added. "Why?"

"I feel her, it's strong."

I heard Silas rush to the bars of his cage quickly before hissing in my direction, "Is she hurt? What are they doing?" His emotions slammed into me, forcing their way inside my mind and body.

"I'll heal her!" Samara growled.

"If they hurt one hair on her head, I swear…" Laz joined.

I nearly doubled over at the force of their worry. Fucking hell. I was highly susceptible to their emotions lately. It had been getting worse the last few days. The last torture session with Bennett nearly ripped the breath from my lungs. I hadn't noticed any fundamental shift in my power since that first day other than the potency of the emotions I felt. I knew that something happened, but so far, all that's changed is that it was getting stronger, and not in the way I'd necessarily prefer. I pressed a hand to my temple and rubbed. It was frustratingly agonizing, feeling everything so intensely all the time. My family's pain during the torture sessions was the one thing that genuinely threatened to topple every ounce of resolve I had.

"Please calm down," I bit back, harsher than I needed to, but I needed them to get a grip on themselves and soon. "You're killing me."

"Sorry," Laz whispered, and I noticed them settle into a calmer latent worry rather than the fierce stabbing concern I'd just felt.

"She's not in pain or afraid. In fact, she's feeling almost hopeful?" I whispered because even though we had been holding onto the clear confidence that we would survive this, hope was still a dangerous thing to harbor.

"Hopeful?" Silas clarified as his emotions returned to his standard tense resting rate.

"She's relieved about something," I added, focusing again on her damn near gleeful emotions now that my coven had settled their own.

"What would she feel relieved about in here?" Laz asked. I shook my head, unable to answer.

"Maybe that Hunter is bringing her back to see us," Samara offered hopefully. She had been the one to benefit the most from Athena's last visit, having fed on her. The moment when Samara fed on her, I felt every second of the euphoric rush. Every ounce of drained blood felt like it ran through my own veins. It was a blinding bloodlust. I had not felt the emotions of a feeding that intensely in my entire existence. It felt like I had been the one whose lips were pressed against her skin, and my fangs that were piercing her arm. But it didn't offer any reprieve from the desperate need I felt. It only made me more ravenous for her.

"Bennett's boy," Silas added. "When we get out of here and start ripping out throats, remind me to start with him."

"He brought Athena to us," Samara countered.

"He captured us," Silas responded.

I felt their blood boiling and their fury beginning to ramp up again. "Please, both of you, stop getting worked up for five goddamn minutes," I exclaimed, pressing my fingers to my temples.

"What's wrong with you?" Laz asked softly after a few moments.

"Nothing," I tossed out. But they weren't having that.

"Tell us the truth, Orpheus," Laz demanded calmly.

"The mate bond amplified my power," I began, rubbing calming little circles into the sides of my skull.

"That's a good thing, right?" Silas asked, but I could feel Samara's pity overpower anything else.

"You're getting overwhelmed by it all, aren't you?" Samara added quietly. I nodded, knowing she couldn't see me, but I didn't want to give voice to the concerns.

"I don't get it. What's going on with your power?" Silas asked with a twinge of worry flaring in his emotions.

"It's like… every radio station in the entire county is playing at full volume simultaneously," I tried to explain. It was a pitiful comparison, but there weren't really words that could accurately describe just how vicious the feelings were when they all flooded in.

At that moment alone, I could feel Athena's relief, my coven's worry and pity, Bennett's fury somewhere in the compound, and various pools of fear, anger, and happiness seeping from each guard within the building—all at once.

"Damn," Silas relented.

"Yes, well, it would help a lot if you could keep yourselves under control and don't go flying off the handle," I nearly begged. I hated how weak my voice sounded. I needed to get a handle on this and fast if I wanted to keep a level head.

"We'll try," Laz promised. "Won't we?" They prompted.

"Well, yeah, but I can't promise anything," Silas said. I sighed softly as I felt the guilt rush through him. He often felt things the strongest of the four of us. I didn't even need to use my ability to know how he was feeling most of the time, but I knew he would try. That was enough for now.

"So, Athena is feeling hopeful. Can you tell why?" Samara offered, bringing us back to the conversation.

"No, but it's strong." I tried to tune out everything else to focus on her. The energy radiating off of her was getting closer. "She's coming this way." Rustling sounds from the other cells echoed as my coven each stepped forward and tried to lean through the bars.

Another set of emotions began to overpower hers as she neared our hallway. This feeling was fueled by anxious nerves but held an undertone of guilt, regret, and determination. The emotions of someone who has done wrong but was fixated on making it right.

The door at the end of the hall slid open quietly. We may never have heard it if it weren't for our enhanced hearing. Someone was being covert. I braced myself for a fight, taking a steadying breath to stave off the torrent of emotions swirling around in my chest. I'm not even sure I knew which emotion was mine anymore.

I couldn't see the door from my position, but I felt her presence when she entered the hallway. Her emotions were so sweet and so vivid. Her hope called to me, sending warmth bubbling through my chest. I wanted her in my arms, in my bed. I wanted her safe.

The second set of emotions was suffocating: anxiety, uncertainty, betrayal, guilt. There was something almost desperate about the way this person's emotions swirled about the room. I gripped my chest, taking a steadying breath and forcing this new onslaught of feelings to subside, but it wouldn't settle. Whoever was accompanying Athena was overwhelmed. And so was I.

When Athena came into view, a sob lodged itself in my parched throat. She looked tired, but the smile plastered on her face outshone the very moon. Her eyes latched onto mine, and she broke into a sprint, tears streaming down her face. She crossed the painted line on the floor and snaked her arms through the bars to embrace me. The weight of her relief flooded me as her skin touched mine. Her heat warmed me soul-deep, and I basked in her comfort like a cat in the sunlight. In her arms, just for a moment, I didn't feel the assaulting emotions quite as strongly, as if her presence could quiet the torrent of swirling feelings prodding to enter my mind.

"I missed you," she whispered, pressing a soft kiss against the bare skin just below.

I couldn't respond. There weren't enough words. Instead, I pressed a kiss to her exposed neck, intimately aware of the way her blood ran just beneath the surface but not feeling hungry in the slightest.

She pulled back and offered me a soft glance of love before continuing down the line to greet her other mates. However brief, their reunions were filled with relief and warmth. I felt every second of them. It was all so potent I felt claustrophobic for the briefest of moments, surrounded on all sides by the wall of their feelings. Shaking my head, I pulled my eyes from the reunions and shut them tightly, hoping to find a reprieve from it all.

When I opened them again, I saw the little Hunter boy standing anxiously against the wall opposite us. His hands were nervously shoved in his pockets, and he frequently glanced over his shoulder at the entrance to our little torture cavern.

"What are you doing, Hunter?" I asked, drawing his nervous eyes to mine.

He sighed, pressing his back against the wall. "I'm fixing my mistake."

Silas scoffed. "A mistake? Typical Hunter logic, you kidnap and torture us and call it a simple mistake."

"I am going to get all of you out of here," the Hunter said, and I felt the wave of hope crash into me from all sides.

"Why?" Samara asked tentatively. I watched as Athena stepped toward the Hunter and felt an involuntary growl build in my chest.

"Because I'm not my father," he replied, casting a forlorn look at Athena. Twinges of guilt radiated from him in vicious strokes.

Interesting.

"How do we know it's not a trap?" Silas barked in anger.

"You outnumber me, and you're vampires. If this were a trap, it'd be a pretty stupid one," he claimed, and I felt his fear. He was worried, scared. He was telling the truth.

"Archer," Athena whispered, crossing the distance to him. "We need to go."

He nodded, swallowing the lump in his throat.

"I'm going to get you out of here, but I can't do that if you kill me," he pleaded.

"No promises," Silas seethed.

Athena moved back to Silas and pushed a hand through the bars, instantly calming him. "Just let him do this for us," she begged.

The Hunter, Archer, moved forward tentatively, his eyes glued to the painted line on the floor as he approached cautiously. He held his hand up, a key within his grasp, and I simultaneously saw the fear in his eyes. I heard the gasp escape his lips as he stepped across the line toward my cage.

I waited patiently, watching him with darkened eyes as he unlocked the lock and opened the bars.

Suddenly, there was nothing between me and the Hunter who captured us. There was no weapon, no holy water, no garlic, nobody to stop me. I heard his heart race as the blood pumped beneath his skin. I could have his blood in my system in an instant. I could bleed him dry and escape this place with my family in the time it took him to blink.

I could.

I flicked my eyes to Athena, who stood and watched with a nervousness swirling around her. She didn't want me to hurt this Hunter… Archer. And so, for her, I wouldn't. I stepped past the pale figure who had locked his eyes on me in fear and swept up my mate in my arms as Archer moved to Samara's cage.

Athena melted into my arms as if she belonged there, and her lips crashed into mine, and I drank her kiss as if it were the only thing standing between me and death. Because she did, and she was. My hands encircled her waist, ignoring the temptation to explore every inch of her and kiss away each painful reminder of our time apart. When she pulled back, her green eyes bore into mine.

"I missed you," she whispered.

Love.

That's what I was feeling. It was so potent, so clear…. so overwhelming. I doubled over, hands shooting to my temples as if my fingertips could keep my brain from exploding.

"Orpheus, what's wrong?" Athena's voice broke through the haze just as Samara's hands touched my shoulders.

"You're ok, you're ok," Samara whispered to me as she let her healing power travel through my bloodstream. I wasn't injured physically, but I'd be lying if I didn't admit that her healing balm dulled the raging headache to a low thrum of pain. I stood and met Samara's eyes. Nodding my thanks, she smiled before turning and hugging Athena and indulging in her own little reunion.

Archer released Laz, who gave him a less-than-friendly gaze before rushing to Athena. When Archer reached Silas' enclosure, I stepped forward, feeling my brother's anger and fury seeping through his pores.

"Silas,' I warned as Archer unlocked the last lock. Silas rushed through the bars and had Archer up against the opposite wall by his throat instantly. Archer's fear coiled around my throat as if it were me that Silas held captive in his grasp.

"Give me one good reason you deserve to breathe," Silas seethed.

Athena rushed forward, but Samara managed to hold her shoulder. Silas would never hurt her, but he was unpredictable when he was like this, and the fact that he was starving was only another reason she should stay back just until we could calm him down.

Archer's hands came up to hold onto Silas' arms, and as he struggled for air, I found myself unable to take a full breath either. "I…" he started. "I can't.." He finished defeat in his tone and his eyes. Guilt again filled my senses.

"Put him down, Silas," I ordered in a forceful whisper. My tone left no room for argument. I wasn't asking. I was demanding as the leader of this Coven. Silas knew that by the annoyance that flooded his emotions as he let Archer's feet hit the ground again.

The Hunter rubbed his throat and forced in gasps of air. "I want to help you. I know it doesn't make any sense, but.." He looked toward Athena with an air of familiarity. If I couldn't tell that he wasn't feeling an ounce of romantic feelings toward her, jealousy may have reared its ugly head. There was undoubtedly a type of care in his gaze that was perplexing, but I had no time to analyze that now. "Athena helped me see that my father has been feeding me lies, and you don't deserve to be punished for the lies of a Hunter," he spat. My eyebrows raised in surprise at his vitriolic tone.

"Please, let him help us," Athena begged, stepping forward to rest a hand on

Silas' arm. He captured her lips in a brief but heated kiss before nodding.

"Sorry, bookworm," he whispered into her ear before pulling back and glaring at Archer. "Ok, Hunter. Get us out of here."

Archer nodded, gulping heavily. His fear was potent, and he refused to show us his back. Smart move. "The guards are going to be switching shifts soon. They don't leave any gaps by the door on the main floor anymore," he said, eyeing us. "But there are a few solid minutes when they don't watch the windows on the upper floor during the shift. You up to scaling the wall?" He asked with a bit of teasing as he looked at Athena. Her eyes went wide.

"We've got it," Laz interjected, throwing an arm around Athena's waist and pulling her to their side. "We've got you," they whispered to her. A wave of lust radiated from her, and I cleared my throat as heat coiled in my stomach, pushing away the feeling of her arousal because if I let myself feel it, I'd need to take her right here in this dungeon and we definitely did not have time for that.

"We need to work fast, and we don't have time for mistakes," Archer continued. "I know it's been a while since you were last here, but my father didn't spend that time just waiting for your return. He's been preparing for this. New weapons, new safeguards. If he catches us, he won't let you go."

"What do you need us to do?" Samara asked, always the calm one. I could feel Silas' resentment at being told to follow a Hunter's lead almost as clearly as I felt Athena's hope return. I took steadying breaths. I needed to get a handle on these fucking emotions before I lost my head.

Archer explained his plan, and I listened intently. It was simple enough but needed to be timed precisely, leaving no room for mistakes. We'd make our way to the complex's third floor, then sneak out through the windows in the exercise gym. Apparently, there weren't cameras in the gym, but that didn't account for the cameras in the halls.

"I've disabled the cameras in here and the hall leading to the gym, but they'll notice the looping soon. I'm not the most accomplished hacker. So, we need to move now." Archer stepped toward the door he came from but then quickly spun to face us, realizing he had accidentally turned his back to us.

His anxiety threatened to rage against my chest.

"We're not going to harm you, Hunter. Just get us out of here, and we will be even," I promised, ignoring the glare that Silas was now giving me.

Archer cast his eyes across each of us briefly, landing on Athena. That same strange familiarity washed over his face, but finally, he nodded and turned to lead us from our cages.

My Coven fell into line behind him. Wordlessly, we encircled Athena, protecting her on each side. It felt so right to have her near us again. Even now, I felt the mate bond within my chest thrum with glee at her proximity. I loved hearing her heartbeat despite its quickened rate from the danger surrounding our current task. I tried to focus on her, and only her, but the other emotions surrounding us were so charged and heightened that I was having a hard time focusing on my own breathing, let alone someone else. Instead, I focused on putting one foot in front of the other and keeping Athena safe. I would deal with this new facet of my power when we were safe.

I felt Athena's gaze on the side of my face, and I turned to look at her.

She knew not to speak as we neared the door she had just arrived through, but her eyes asked the unspoken question.

I nodded, trying my best to reassure my mate that I was okay. I didn't need her worrying about me when she needed to focus on keeping herself safe. She gripped my hand in hers and squeezed, and I let her touch ground me the best it could. We reached the door and Archer listened quietly at the iron frame. He pressed his hands against its surface, waiting for the right moment to open. Just as he moved to push through the door, I felt a new set of emotions. Two guards were just beyond the door. I felt them as they strolled through the hall. I sent my hand out, encircling Archer's wrist and holding him back. His heart rate quickened, and his breathing became labored as pure, unbridled fear coursed through him.

His hand shook in my grasp. I saw the beginnings of a panic attack and quickly removed my hand from his wrist and whispered, "Two guards just outside." It took him a moment to calm his breathing, but when he did, he nodded first to me and then to himself. I'd seen that reaction before, in Athena when she had her panic attack back at her bookstore. He had PTSD, and by the way, he was cradling his wrist that held a raised white scar, I knew exactly what had caused it.

A wave of my own guilt ran through me at that thought.

I quickly pushed it down and tuned into the set of emotions beyond the door. I could feel their trajectory clearly, tracking them despite the barrier between us. I guess, in that respect, my newfound amplified powers would be helpful. I just hoped I could keep them from overwhelming me long enough to benefit.

"They've gone around the corner. We're clear," I whispered to the Hunter, and he swallowed the fear, schooling his expression, and moved forward again. We pressed through the door and spilled out into the hallway quietly. Even with my advanced hearing, I could barely hear our footfalls. We'd need to remain as quiet as possible to get out of here undetected. From here, I could feel almost fifty other people in this building. Moving about like ants in a maze. Their emotions called out like beacons. Helpful…and distracting. I focused on our path, trying to scope out who might be crossing us.

Archer led us toward the back staircase for a few painfully tense minutes, his eyes darting to me as we came to each corner for confirmation. I'd offer a tight nod to confirm we were clear, and we'd continue. Never in my life did I think I'd work *with* a Hunter, but Archer didn't seem like the Hunters I'd encountered before. He was different. I wasn't planning on grabbing a beer with him anytime soon, but I'd let him lead us out of here. I'd trust him to do that. I didn't sense an ounce of dishonesty in him, and there was something protective in his gaze when he looked at Athena, which made me want to believe him. It was apparent that Athena did.

When we reached the stairs, Archer glanced at me, and I tried to focus on the beacons of emotions. There were three guards on the next floor, but they weren't near the door to the stairway.

I nodded, and he began to climb.

Step after step, I did my best to remain focused on those three guards. If they took one step toward our direction, I wanted to know about it.

We made it another ten steps up the staircase before I felt it.

Blinding, violent, unrelenting rage.

It burned through my veins like acid, eating away at my very skin. My knees buckled under me, and I collapsed onto the steps. Silas grabbed my shoulders and held me steady before I could slip backward.

The beacons of emotions from the other guards grew, their anger and determination growing stronger with each passing moment. My chest tightened, and I struggled to remain quiet, resisting the urge to scream out and release the tension from the pain building in my body.

I recognized Athena's hushed voice as she spoke to someone, and they responded, but I couldn't drown out my emotions well enough to hear what they had said. There was nothing but rage. I was drowning in it.

Suddenly, her hands came to rest on my cheeks, and I tried to force my eyes open to meet hers, but the pain was too great. Her lips pressed into mine, and I tried to zero in on the place where her skin met mine.

She called out to me in the darkness like a beacon. Like a lighthouse. She was the only thing that could keep me from falling into the deep end. "Be here with me," she demanded against my lips. "Nothing but me and you, Orpheus. Do you hear me? There's nothing but you and me. Drown it all out," she begged. I forced my eyes open to meet hers, finding watery green eyes staring back at me. "Feel me, only me," she cried, bringing my hand to her chest so that I could feel her heartbeat. It was racing but strong and powerful, and I couldn't help but love the way it called to me. "Four things you can see, Orpheus." She commanded, and I felt the corners of my lips try to twitch into a smile before the rage burned another hole in my chest.

"I can't.." I strained.

"Drown it out," she begged.

I shook my head. "I can't." How could I shut out something that felt so overwhelming and all-encompassing?

"Yes, you can!" She whisper-screamed. I heard Archer's voice in the background, but I couldn't feel anything past the fury and my mate's hands on me. "You're stronger than this. You always have been. Drown. Them. Out!"

Her words felt like a crashing window. Shattered pieces of the power in my soul came crashing down in fractals around me. Suddenly, there was only her before me. It was as if a switch had been flipped, instantly dampening the overwhelming surge of emotions that had been bombarding me from all directions. The chaos around me began to lose intensity— like a roaring storm gradually subsiding into a gentle rain.

With each passing moment, the weight of the emotional burden lifted, and I could feel a sense of clarity and lightness washing over me. It was as if a heavy curtain had been drawn, shielding me from the relentless onslaught of feelings that had previously threatened to engulf me. The world's noise faded into the background, replaced by a serene stillness that enveloped me completely.

In that newfound calm, I could finally hear the gentle whisper of my emotions rising to the surface. It was a revelation. For the first time in my second life, it was my emotions and mine alone that swirled within me.

My eyes locked with Athena's, and I pressed a kiss onto her lips, an incredulous laugh slipping through my lips.

"Are you ok?" she asked, a flash of something crossing her face. Worry probably…but I didn't know for sure. I didn't know because I couldn't feel her emotions.

There was peace.

"You helped me turn it off," I whispered, throwing my arms around her waist and pulling her to my chest.

She pressed a kiss to my throat, and I felt the burn of lust build in my lower stomach, making my cock twitch for her, but I pushed that unruly reaction away and stood with her in my arms.

"Sorry," I offered to my coven and Archer, who watched us with rapt attention. I'm ready now. We need to hurry. Someone has realized we're gone."

I felt the power thrum within my chest. It wasn't gone, but I had control over it in ways I never had before. I tested it as we continued up the stairs, switching it on and off. By the time we reached the landing on the second floor, it was as easy as breathing. I smiled at Athena before telling Archer that the hall was clear and sliding the overwhelming power off, placing those painful emotions into a box and sliding it away until I needed to call on it again.

Athena had saved me in ways I'd never knew I could be saved. Her love set me free from the mental cage I had been forced to occupy for centuries. She had given me more than just a reprieve from the pain, but she's offered me a type of control I'd been craving. She was saving me over and over again, and when we got out of here safely, I was going to do everything I could to show her how thankful I was.

SILAS

TWELVE

I was going to kill Orpheus when we got out of here.

Who the hell did he think he was, promising the Hunter that we wouldn't kill him? I'd been planning and running through the very detailed and excruciating ways I had planned to make this fucker pay for what he put us through, for what he put Athena through. I was going to enjoy exacting my revenge slowly and violently. And this fucking suit and tie-wearing jackass stole that chance from me.

I was fuming as we made our way through the halls, and I was fuming as we climbed the stairs. Hell, I was fuming when Orpheus nearly slipped and fell. There was a split second when I considered not catching him. We were only halfway up the staircase. He wouldn't die. It would just hurt him—a lot. And if you asked me, he deserved it.

But he's my fucking brother, and I fucking love him for some stupid ass reason, so I caught him before he went headfirst down the stairwell. He had the audacity to be all in pain and make me worry for him…the fucking jackass.

My eyes watched the little Hunter like a hawk. He was jittery, and I was ready to take him out the second he showed even the slightest sign of betraying us. I couldn't look at his stupid ass face without remembering the way I was frozen in my body as he hauled me into the back of his truck.

Orpheus may look at the Hunter and see our ticket out, but I look at him as I see the reason we need the ticket in the first place. I was really looking forward to ripping out his intestines and hanging him from the rafters… dammit. Stupid Romanian bastard always ruins my fun.

Archer and Orpheus worked in tandem, like old fucking buddies or some shit, to navigate the halls toward the gym. We heard shouts echoing through the halls, but luckily for us, they seemed to be headed for the first floor. They wouldn't expect us to escape through the second-floor window. It was a good plan. Even though he was a stupid fucking Hunter. The alarms began blaring, and suddenly, the lights dimmed, and an eerie, almost green light flooded the hall. I pressed in closer to Athena and watched our backs as our eyes attempted to adjust to the color, but it hurt. The color was bright and invasive. It felt like I was staring directly into sunlight.

"What the fuck?" I cursed quietly, rubbing my eyes.

"It's designed specifically to affect a vampire's eyesight," Archer explained quickly. "I warned you, he's prepared for this. We need to hurry."

I wanted to punch him, but I couldn't fucking see him. Douchebag.

"We can't see," Laz exclaimed.

"Athena, can you lead them?" Archer asked, and I felt her hand come to rest on my arm, sending calming waves through me.

"Hold onto me," she whispered, and I felt my coven gather closer to her. We were rushing through the hall now, and I hated the way my blindness made me feel so helpless. The alarm was high-pitched to mess with my hearing, but I could still smell them. They weren't onto our trail… yet.

"In here, come on," Archer said, and I heard him push a door open. His footfalls echoed in the room, and I knew we had reached the gym. The smell of sweat invaded my nostrils. The light was diluted in this room, just enough that I could make out shapes around us. "The windows are on the other side. Hurry!" Archer took off across the floor, and Athena did her best to keep each of us close as she raced after him. I listened as Archer opened the window, and fresh air hit my skin for the first time since we were abducted. My heart raced, and I felt agonizing hope fill my chest. We would be free soon. I hadn't let myself believe in the possibility until this very moment. This close to the window, the green light was weak enough for my vision to return to me at mostly total capacity. It was nighttime outside, and the moonlight poured in, washing away the green. Good. That would help us disappear.

"Come on, climb out," Archer ordered, and I ignored the urge to tell him to shut the fuck up and stop telling me what to do because, as furious as I was, he was the reason I could taste the freedom beyond the window.

"Athena, go," I said, leading her toward the window.

"Um... Maybe you should go first so someone can catch me if- Well." Her eyes looked out and down toward the ground outside the window. It was a drop that would be a piece of cake for us but could kill a human being.

"Laz, Samara, go out on either side. You can help her down when we send her out," Orpheus demanded.

"I can't leave her..." Samara started, and tears had formed in her eyes. She was terrified of leaving Athena behind because the last time one of us was left behind... I gripped Athena's hand in mine.

"I will protect her, Samara. Get out there and be ready to jump. I have her." I promised her. Samara and I shared a brief moment before she nodded and slipped out of the window with Laz close on her heels. Losing Alora had nearly broken us both, and I would never let another one of us be lost in this fucking building.

"Silas, get her out of here," Orpheus looked to me, watching the door from which we came, basked in green light. His jaw tensed.

"They're coming, aren't they?" I whispered low enough that only he could hear me. He nodded.

"Go, get out there. I'll send her out. I can blend in if we're not out in time." I could see he wanted to argue, but we didn't have time for that, so he pressed a kiss to Athena's cheek and offered a quick nod to Archer before following Laz and Samara out onto the ledge. I was lifting Athena toward the window when the doors to the gym slammed open. My muscles tensed, and I conjured the only image I could, holding onto Athena tightly and pressing her to my back as I turned to face the incoming guards. I felt my skin tingle as my disguise formed, and I heard Archer inhale sharply beside me in shock.

"What the fuck are you doing here, Bennett?" One of the guards bellowed as he approached. His eyes landed on me, and he shook his head. "Sorry, sir. I didn't realize he was with you."

"Are you going to stand there and berate my son, or are you going to find those fucking vampires?" I called out, hating how Bennett's voice felt in my throat.

"You told us to check this floor," the guard questioned.

"I also told you to find the bloodsuckers. Do I need to ask you again?" I felt Athena press her face into my back, and I tried my best to hide her from view.

"Who is that?" One of the other guards asked, leaning to see around me. I took a step forward, prepared to rip each of their throats out, but then Archer stepped forward and pulled Athena with him. I was a fraction of a second away from turning my fury back on him, but then my eyes landed on Athena, or I guess I should say, the random person who stood in Athena's spot.

Confusion washed over me as I took in her appearance. Her long red hair was cropped short and had a dirty blonde tint. Her ordinarily soft features were angular and sharp. Brown eyes covered her green orbs, and her body was plump and thick. I shook my head, trying to make sense of what I was seeing.

"New recruit," Archer said, showing off the 'not-Athena," who looked equally perplexed. She didn't seem to notice that she looked nothing like herself. Good, if she did, she may not be able to hold in the shock that I was now fighting against.

"Now, are you going to stand there like fucking idiots, or are you going to follow orders?" I bellowed. The guards nodded, agreeing quickly and backing out toward the door. We watched them go, and I took a moment to breathe before letting the facade fall away. When I did, Athena's visage also melted away, revealing her.

"Neat trick," Archer whispered before ushering Athena, who was now looking much more Athena-like, toward the window.

She looked dazed but went to climb through. "Wait, Archer. What will happen if they find out you're behind this?" Her tone was full of worry.

"I'll be fine. I'm just glad I could do this for you," he whispered, and I saw him brush away a tear that slid down his cheek.

"Come on, bookworm, we gotta go." I helped her through the window, and she watched Archer.

"Thank you, Archer," she whispered before stepping out onto the ledge and into the waiting arms of her other mates. I turned back to the Hunter and scowled.

"This doesn't make up for what you did," I spat.

He nodded. "I know."

I nodded once, the most acknowledgment he would get out of me, and moved to slip out the window. I was halfway out when the door to the gym opened again.

"What the fuck have you done, Archer?" Bennett's voice echoed through the room, and I hurried to slide out the window. Samara and Laz were already helping Athena down the ledge, and Orpheus was ahead of them, watching our exit path. I turned my head back to the Hunter. He backed away as his father and the guard that accompanied him advanced.

"You've been lying to me, to all of us." Archer reached for the stake in his waistband. Shock flooded me. Would he actually use it against his father? Was he really so opposed to what his family did here that he'd fight him?

"You ruined everything," Bennett said, indicating with a nod to the guard at his side. The guard grunted, rushing forward and grabbing Archer in a less-than-friendly headlock. Archer cried out and tried to wrestle free from the hold.

"I should let this guard fucking kill you for your treason," Bennett seethed, eyes wide and hair wild. He was a madman, angered and unstable.

The guard let his fist fly, a punch landing on Archer's face. I smelled the blood as it poured from his now broken nose. I felt my shift just under the surface, and I barely held it together.

"Silas, come on," Orpheus called from the ground below. His voice came to me through a haze of hunger and fury.

I watched through red-tinted eyes as Archer attempted to stand up, but the guard was faster, sending another punch at him as his father watched on. This one landed with a sickening crunch, and more blood filled the air. I was damn-near ravenous. My hands gripped the windowsill, and I watched as the Hunter who captured us took blow after blow, ordered by the Hunter who tortured us.

"Silas, get your ass down here," Samara seethed. "We need to go." She was afraid, understandably.

"Bennett's got the kid," I whispered, knowing they could hear me.

"Fuck," Orpheus exclaimed.

"What's wrong? What is it?" Athena's worried tone broke through my near shift and cleared my head. The monster slipped back into the shadows of my mind as I watched Archer stand to face his father.

"You made it all up, Dad. All of it," he spat, blood pouring down his chin.

"You don't know what the hell you're talking about," Bennett yelled, watching as his guard dropped a kick in the kid's stomach, sending him toppling backward.

My fists clenched.

"What is happening up there? What's going on? Talk to me!" Athena begged her other mates.

"Archer's dad found him," Laz answered softly. Damn them and their big mouth.

"Is he ok?" She asked with worry in her tone.

"We have guards headed this way," Orpheus declared through gritted teeth.

"Is Archer ok?" Athena demanded.

"We need to go," Orpheus said, reaching for her, but she pulled back.

"Not until I know he's alright," she stated.

I focused again on the Hunter, who was on the ground in a heap, blood pooling on the floor below him.

"You're worthless, you know that?" Bennett exclaimed, stepping forward. I ducked further onto the ledge so he wouldn't see me. "You always have been. You and you're fucking naivete. You have no idea what you just did. No fucking clue who you just released back into the world."

"Yes, I do," Archer said weakly, lifting his battered head to face his father. "I know exactly who I just released back into the world. I know exactly who she is. And so do you!"

My brows furrowed at that, confusion coursing through me, but Bennett understood the vague confession. The color drained from his face, and his steps faltered. What the fuck was that supposed to mean? Did he mean Samara or Athena? What the hell was going on? On the ground, Orpheus was trying desperately to get Athena to run while she struggled in his hold. We were running out of time.

"You will have to answer to Galvin, and I won't be able to protect you from that. Do you understand what I'm saying?" Bennett seethed, nodding again to the guard at his side, who landed another kick to Archer's chest. He curled around the hit and cried out in pain.

"Was that him?" Athena cried out. Her voice traveled to my ears, but luckily, Bennett didn't seem to hear it. She needed to be careful.

"You'd let Galvin kill me?"

My breath caught in my throat. Based on Archer's state, he wasn't too far from death already.

"I'd have no choice." With a frown, Bennett shook his head, dismissing the guard. Together, they turned on their heels and rushed out of the gym, leaving Archer, broken and bloody, on the floor. The Hunter's breathing became shallow as his body went slack.

In all my years of existence, I'd made a point of living my life to protect others from those who sought to hurt them. I'd stop monsters, far more evil than I, from taking what didn't belong to them, be it sex, skin, or blood. I'd fight for those who couldn't fight for themselves or had fought and lost. It was ingrained in who I was to be the silent protector, even when I felt like I couldn't. Even when it didn't make sense. Even when I fucking hated them.

That's why I found myself climbing back into the window, despite the protests from the ground, scooping the unconscious boy in my arms, and then taking the jump from the window in one leap.

Looks like we're taking the fucking Hunter with us.

Great.

ATHENA

THIRTEEN

The moment Silas landed on the ground near us with Archer in tow, the panic that had been building began to subside, only to ramp up again once I saw the state of the man I once considered a friend. He had saved us, he had set us free, and he'd almost died because of it. Guilt threatened to topple me over. I didn't realize I had been crying until the salted liquid painted my lips.

"We need to go, Athena. Please, we don't have time." Orpheus begged me harshly, and I knew he wouldn't use that tone unless necessary. I nodded, trying to pry my eyes from Archer's limp body, and climbed onto Orpheus's back. "Make sure he doesn't have anything that can be tracked." Silas and Samara tag teamed, rifling through his belongings, tossing Archer's phone on the ground, and smashing it. They nodded to us where we stood.

Then we were off.

Orpheus was fast. In the darkness of the night, I couldn't make out a single shape as the world around us blurred. I felt my mates running alongside us, but I couldn't see them in the kaleidoscope of air and darkness. With each stride away from the Hunters' compound, I felt relief replacing the fear and pain. I let the gentle sway of Orpheus' steps calm my racing heart. We survived—all of us. My heart constricted as I thought of Archer's poor, battered face. His father had done that? How could he do that to his own son?

Those who are meant to protect us can do the most harm.

The small voice in the back of my mind reminded me as a flash of perfect teeth and combed hair threatened to replace the forest's darkness with the memory of his face. I closed my eyes and pushed back against the thought of him. He had been a frequent visitor in my consciousness this past week. The feeling of being trapped, the helplessness…it all felt so familiar. I couldn't help but slip into those waking nightmares of when his calloused hands trailed my skin when his wicked lips took from me what I was unwilling to give.

I took a deep breath and focused on the feeling of my mate beneath me. His muscular body was chilled, and I let the cold comfort wash away his sweaty memory. Soon enough, I managed to force my stepfather back into the box reserved for him in the corner of my mind.

I don't know how long we ran, but I felt Orpheus's stride stagger. He was putting on a brave face, but I saw it in the way his shoulders tightened and the crease in his brow.

He was weak.

"Stop," I said into his ear.

"Not yet," he replied, the fatigue evident in his voice.

"Stop right now, Orpheus," I demanded, and he slowed his footfalls with a sigh. When we came to a stop, I slid off his back and let my feet hit the ground. I didn't miss how his body seemed relieved not to carry the extra weight.

"We can't stop, Athena. We're not out of danger yet. These woods are all theirs," he began, but I put a hand up to stop him. I heard Laz, Samara, and Silas come to a stop behind me as well.

When I turned to look at them, I saw it for the first time. The effect these last few days had had on them. They weren't ok. They weren't desiccating into nothingness, but they were weak and tired and hungry. I stepped forward, seeing Silas' near-red eyes as he held Archer's bleeding body in his arms.

"You need to feed," I whispered.

"We need to get out of here," Orpheus argued, strained though at the prospect of feeding.

"We'll be quick, but you need the strength," I said, stepping forward and offering my throat to him. His eyes darkened with hunger and lust, and his tongue came out to wet his lips before he tore his eyes from the pulse at my neck.

"We might lose control," he pleaded.

"You won't," I responded, grabbing Samara's hand and bringing it to my chest, letting her feel my heartbeat. "Samara has kept me strong. I can do this. Please let me do this for you."

Samara let out a whimper, a delicious sound that I couldn't wait to taste when we were safe, but now she needed something else from me, and I needed to give it.

"Darlin'," Laz warned as I reached for them, bringing them to my side and offering my wrist. Their eyes locked on my pulse, and they began to shift.

"Silas, please," I beckoned him forward. He was so close to losing his control that it didn't take much pushing for him to set the bloody Archer down on a nearby patch of soft ground and step toward me, pressing his front to my back and claiming my throat with his fangs. I bit my lip to stifle the moan as the pressure built. It was an otherworldly experience, having him drink from me. Samara pressed a gentle kiss against the inside of my forearm before sinking her teeth into the flesh and drinking. My head fell back as heat pooled in my core. Laz licked my wrist with their tongue, which made the cool night air tingle against my skin. I shivered in anticipation, but then they were biting down, taking languid sips of my blood.

I felt like I was on fire, a burning inferno of passion, as my eyes locked onto Orpheus, who was entirely shifted. His sharp ears and bright red eyes had once terrified me but now made me feel coveted, desired, and protected. He stalked forward and claimed the side of my throat opposite Silas and pressed his body to my front. Once his fangs were inserted into my skin, I couldn't stifle the sound anymore. I groaned as an orgasm ripped through me, sending shockwaves to every extremity. They pulled slow and steady gulps of my blood into their mouths, and I writhed in their hold, gasping with release.

Laz was the first to pull away, followed by Samara. Their vampire forms drifted away to reveal their heated gazes. Silas released his hold on my throat, licking the wound and sending a jolt of pleasure directly to my core. Orpheus took a moment longer to release his hold, but soon enough, he was drawing back, using the back of his hand to wipe the excess blood from his lips. The sight of my blood on his skin shouldn't be as tempting as it was. Unfortunately, I didn't have time to explore his mouth with mine as I desired.

"Are you ok?" Orpheus asked tentatively.

I nodded, smiling. "I'm perfect."

He released a sigh before offering me his back again. I climbed on and watched as Silas retrieved Archer.

"Samara, can you help him?" I asked. She pressed a soft kiss to my lips.

"I healed him as much as I could on the run here. He's alive and stable. I'll do more when we get where we're going." She smiled softly, and I instantly felt better.

"Speaking of, where are we going?" I asked as we began to run again.

"I've been preparing for this for a long time, little nymph. I knew someday they'd catch us again, and we'd need to escape," Orpheus replied in an even tone despite the incredible speed at which we traveled. Even the minuscule amount of blood he took was already making a huge difference in his strength.

I held him tighter, hating how much fear they had been living in for all these years.

"I have a safehouse about an hour's run from here. We'll be safe there until we figure out what to do." He squeezed my hand, and that was enough to calm my nerves as he continued his trek through the forest.

Sometime later - it may have been an hour, but I had no way of knowing for sure - Orpheus slowed to a light jog. "Are we here?" I asked.

"Nearly," he replied softly. "We could have been here earlier, but I wanted to double back and cover our trail."

I nodded.

Right. We needed to cover our trail because we were on the run… from Vampire Hunters. I felt my stomach flip as the reality of our situation settled on me. However, I didn't have time to dwell on that feeling because the dense canopy of trees suddenly gave way, revealing a small meadow nestled within the heart of the wilderness. Moonlight filtered through the gaps in the foliage, casting patterns of muted light and shadow across the vibrant carpet of wildflowers that blanketed the expanse. A narrow trail wound its way through the meadow, leading toward a seemingly abandoned two-story cabin standing at the edge of the clearing. Despite the wear and tear evident in its weathered exterior, there was an undeniable warmth to the rustic structure.

Above the cabin, the canopy of leaves stretched out like a protective shield, enveloping the area in a cocoon of privacy and seclusion. It was as though the forest itself conspired to keep us concealed from prying eyes, both on the ground and in the sky.

Approaching the cabin, I felt a sense of tranquility wash over me at the promise of safety within the cabin walls. Orpheus did not stop to let me admire the sight for any longer before sprinting up the steps with me firmly attached to his back. I heard the others follow closely, and within a few moments, we were all locked safely inside the cabin's living area. A faint scent of aged wood and must served as a reminder of the cabin's long solitude and lack of use. Yet, despite its apparent disuse, the cabin's interior seemed prepared and ready, as if it had been patiently awaiting our arrival. That thought sent a wave of sadness to my heart. How long had my mates been waiting for this moment? Had they ever considered there would be a time when they didn't need this safe house? Or did they always know they'd be here someday?

The main living area had sturdy, well-crafted wooden furniture draped with dust covers. A plush sofa and armchairs sat around a stone fireplace, their cushions invitingly plump, which only reminded me of my exhaustion. A thick rug lay beneath, its intricate patterns softened by time and wear.

Orpheus set me on my feet and helped me steady myself as feeling returned to the tired extremities before he returned to the door. Beneath his touch, I noticed a modern element that seemed out of place amidst the rustic charm of the cabin—a security system. A keypad lock adorned the door, its sleek design starkly contrasting the weathered wood around it. As Orpheus armed the alarm, I watched and heard the system whir to life. Motion sensors dotted the room's corners, their small lights flashing to confirm they were on and ready. Now that I was looking, I saw several cameras littering the space, and I knew that if I had paid enough attention, I would have seen them outside as well. I eyed the camera that was aimed at the front door. Its unblinking lens was a silent sentinel watching over us. I felt that wave of relief course through me.

Once Orpheus was satisfied with the arming of our safehouse, he turned to face us where we stood. My eyes drifted across the haggard faces of my mates, watching them as they let the weight of the last few hours, especially the previous weeks, settle over them. We stood together in a heavy silence, each fighting our internal struggles against the demons within. Every dreadful moment of the past two weeks seemed to seep into our very bones, leaving an indelible mark on our souls. There wasn't a doubt in my mind that we would remember what had occurred for as long as we drew breath. Some of us were fortunate enough to escape physically unscathed, but the scars ran deep, and they always would. I understand intimately that scars, whether seen or unseen, have a way of persisting.

"What is this place, Orpheus?" Laz asked calmly.

"A safe house," he replied.

"Obviously, but since when did you have this?" Silas interjected.

"Since about two months after we escaped the last time." The words hung in the air, and the others all inhaled a shaky breath.

"Why didn't you tell us?" Silas asked an edge of anger in his tone.

"Because you all wanted to believe that we were safe, but I knew we weren't." Orpheus ran a hand through his hair, and I took this moment to really look at him. He was still in his suit pants, but his button-down shirt was tattered, ripped, and singed. My chest tightened at the thought of what they had to endure there. Again.

"There is a state-of-the-art security system, with alarms for a mile perimeter. The kitchen is fully stocked with blood, but I do have some non-perishables as well," he added, tipping his head toward me. "Each bedroom has clothes in our sizes," he continued, trying not to make eye contact with any of us. Laz was slack-jawed. "You'll need to share with Samara." He shot me an apologetic look.

"Thank you," Samara said eventually, her voice hoarse and tired. "Thank you for this, Orpheus."

Then Samara began to cry. My chest ached as she sobbed. I rushed to her, pulling her gently into my arms, and she nestled her head into my neck and folded her arms around me. The return to the Hunter's cages was obviously hard on each of them, but I knew this memory held a special kind of torture for her. My heart broke for Alora, the love of my mate's life. Oh, how I wished I could have known her. Could have saved her. "I'm so sorry," I whispered against Samara's hair, pressing delicate kisses to the top of her head.

"Silas, get Archer set up in the basement There's a couch down there... and some extra security measures," I heard Orpheus order, and I sighed. They would, of course, be wary of the man who captured them, but at least they were helping him.

That's how I knew, once and for all, beyond a shadow of the doubt, that the Hunters tried to plant in my mind that my Wanderers were not the monsters that Nameless believed they were.

Silas and Laz ventured toward a door that led to what I assumed was the basement Orpheus mentioned and disappeared with a still unconscious Archer. I heard Orpheus take some steps further into the house, leaving Samara and me to have this moment alone. We sunk down to our knees on the wooden floor, and still, she cried into my arms.

"I was so afraid," she whispered. I ran a hand along her spine, applying just enough comforting pressure.

"We're ok," I replied because it was true. We had made it out—all of us.

"I felt like I couldn't breathe, like at any moment they would take another member of my family from me." Samara sat back on her heels and placed a palm on my cheek. I was mesmerized by her dark eyes glistening with moisture. Despite the hardness of her features, she was stunning and seemed so soft and vulnerable in the gentle moonlight.

"I know." My heart constricted. I couldn't imagine the pain she had been in, feeling the memories flashing back, seeing the same scenarios play out, unable to stop them. "The memories are the hardest part," I added, swallowing hard.

She leaned forward and pressed the softest kiss to my forehead.

"You made it bearable," she promised, and I loved the way her eyes captured mine like she saw so deep within me that my soul was laid bare before her. "Thank you."

I ran my thumb along her bottom lip, loving how her cold breath sent shivers of anticipation down my spine. "No, thank you. You kept me healthy. You healed me."

"We healed each other," she admitted, and I ushered my agreement in the form of a soft kiss pressed against her parted lips. She moaned slightly as I drank her kiss. I pulled back, locking eyes with my mate again, and the mark on my wrist thrummed with energy.

"Why don't we clean up, and then I'll see what else I can do for Archer?" Samara offered, and the mention of Archer had a wave of guilt cresting.

"He's hurt because he helped us," I whispered, a tear sliding down my cheek. Samara caught it with her finger.

"He's alive because he helped us," she replied quietly. "I'm not sure Silas or Orpheus would have let him breathe if he hadn't."

I nodded. I figured as much. Hell, in those first few days, I may have killed him myself if it meant I could be free again.

"He'll be ok. We'll make sure of it. Like I said, he's stable." She pressed her promise in the form of a kiss on my lips, and I leaned into it hungrily. Feeling my core tighten at the feel of her lips against mine.

She pulled back, smirking. "Let's go take a shower, Athena."

I shook my head. "I need to call my grandma. She's probably so worried." My heart constricted. "I'm all she has left." A tear slid down my cheek, and Samara caught it with her thumb. "And Davia, too! And what about the cops that are looking into us? I mean, disappearing in the middle of an investigation is pretty suspicious." Another thought occurred to me, and my stomach sank. "What if they found Greg, and he told them what I did to him?" I was fully panicking now. Samara's hands came to my shoulders and squeezed.

"Breathe, sweetheart."

I tried, but inhaling felt impossible.

"Look at me, and breathe," she commanded, and I finally locked my eyes on hers and took a long, languid breath.

"There is a lot to figure out, there are a lot of questions, but they can wait for tomorrow."

I started to protest, but she shut me up with a kiss.

"It can all wait for tomorrow, my love. You've been through something horrible and need a moment to process that."

I nodded, not sure I fully believed her, but I felt the calm start to wash over me.

"So, my beautiful, perfect mate. Shower with me." Her words held a wicked edge that I instantly felt guilty about being excited about, but I quickly squashed that guilt.

We'd just been through the unthinkable and came out the other side. We're alive. We're safe. For now, at least. I deserve a moment of indulgence. She's right. These problems would still be here tomorrow.

Samara stood and took my hand, leading me through the rest of the unfamiliar space. Once we reached the top of the stairs, I let her lead me to the master bathroom. Although to call it 'master' anything felt disjointed, seeing as it was a short room housing a slightly larger than small clawfoot tub and a curtain that hung haphazardly from the ceiling. I didn't care, though. The promise of running water and my naked mate was too great a distraction. The door closed behind us, and Samara slowly reached for the hem of my shirt. I was instantly aware of just how long I'd been wearing this same shirt and cringed. I hope she could peel it off my skin without it sticking. She didn't seem to have the same reservations I did because as the shirt was lifted above my head, her eyes scanned my body hungrily.

"Do you know how beautiful you are, Athena?" She asked, trailing a finger along the waistband of my pants. I groaned at the pure need that raced through me at her touch. My head lulled back as she slid the pants down my legs, tugging my panties with them. I didn't have a moment to feel self-conscious about my current state of hygiene because she was up instantly, leading me to take a careful step into the claw foot tub.

"You're joining me, right?" I nearly begged as she stepped back. She smiled and reached for the hem of her ruined sundress, pulling it off her body in one move. I felt my jaw loosen as I took in the image of her perfect naked body. Her breasts were perky, and the nipples pebbled in desire. Her long legs were like roadmaps that led to my favorite destination. I might have moaned.

She stepped into the tub with me, pulling the curtain closed around us, offering us both an air of privacy. The moment the water hit our bodies, we both sighed in contentment. It was chilly, but honestly, I didn't mind the cold temperature anymore—not with my mate's ice-cold hands running along my body.

I let her hands explore the plane of my stomach as I let my hands get tangled in her dark, naturally curly hair. "Let me wash your hair," I asked, and Samara smiled. She handed me a bottle from the shelf, and I got to work, lathering my hands in the glorious-smelling soap. It smelled of lavender and sea. I ran my hands delicately through her hair, listening to her soft instructions on washing her hair properly. She groaned as I took my time with each curl. When I held her back so she could lean back and rinse the soap from her scalp, her hips pressed against my own, and I eagerly pressed back, my needy clit begging for friction.

She stepped back, earning her a frustrated groan, but she only smiled and got to work on my own ratted locks. Her magical hands made a miracle of my hair, easing out the tangles with gentle fingers. I pulled the body wash from the shelf and took a dollop in the palm of my hand. I offered her the same, and she smiled, putting her hand out, palm up for me.

Our hands quickly found each other's bodies and moved in gentle, soap-covered circles across our skin. I lathered her body up, staring at her shoulders, her chest, moving gently to her sides, then brushing ever so slightly against her hardened nipples. She inhaled sharply and paused her own exploration of my body to close her eyes and enjoy my touch. I circled her nipples with my fingers, working slowly and sensually despite the growing pit of need in my core. I pressed a kiss to her exposed throat, and she let her hands wrap around my waist.

My fingers drifted south, exploring every inch of her perfect body until I reached the apex of her thighs. I spent a few moments genuinely lathering the soap onto her body, but I didn't ignore the way her chest rose and fell with the friction I was providing. Once I was content and rinsed her body under the stream of water, I found her clit with my index finger and stroked it.

"Athena," she moaned, and I felt invincible. My name on her lips was something I could never get enough of. I slid two fingers into her pussy, loving the way her core tightened around me.

She gasped, and I took the moment to capture her mouth in a kiss. I drank her moans as I pumped my fingers into her over and over again. Her hands came to a rest on my breasts, and I sighed with pleasure as she caught my nipples between her thumb and forefingers and hardened them to a point.

"Fuck me with those fingers," she commanded in a soft tone, and I obliged instantly, picking up my pace and letting my thumb find her clit as I continued. Her breathing ramped up, and she bucked against my hand.

"You look so beautiful when you're coming," I whispered against her throat before taking a bite of the skin there, and she detonated around my fingers. I felt her walls clamp around me as I drew out the last bits of her release. Her fingers had climbed to my shoulders as she held on for dear life. When her breathing returned to normal, I slid my fingers from her pussy and couldn't resist the temptation to taste them. I slid my fingers into my mouth and groaned as her sweet taste invaded my tastebuds. I was so lost to the taste of her that I didn't notice she had dropped to her knees before me until I felt her cold breath on my sensitive clit. My eyes flashed open, but I left my fingers in my mouth as she positioned my legs where she needed them.

The first draw of her tongue through my folds was nothing short of pure euphoria. I gasped, gripping the top of her head to steady myself against the onslaught of passion. My legs were weak as she devoured my pussy. Her tongue danced in sinfully intricate movements along my soaking wet slit. I whispered her name softly, like a prayer, and she groaned as her tongue assaulted my clit with blinding need. The vibration was enough to make my heart race, my breathing came in rapid spurts, and I felt the orgasm cresting as my mate consumed me.

Her fingers slid into my aching pussy, and her tongue continued its devious attention on my clit, and I felt as if I were flying. Floating above my body, looking down at this sinful and stunning moment of passion.

The muscles in my stomach contracted, telling me I was close, and I whispered in a panted breath, "Don't stop."

She took that moment to slide one of her hands through my slick folds and back even further, teasing the entrance to my tight hole, and I inhaled sharply at the slight bite of anticipation. She slid the finger in, and I moaned at the fullness as she expertly worked me.

Her tongue was on my clit, her fingers were in my pussy, and another finger was pressing into my ass, and I fell apart. I saw stars as the climax crashed into me. Samara didn't pause to let me ride the wave, instead pushing up into me with a punishing pace as her tongue sucked my clit into her mouth. I screamed her name and tried to pull my body away from hers as the tightness built further in my core. She didn't let up, relentlessly pounding into me and torturing my clit. "Please," I begged, unsure if I was begging for her to stop and let me recover from the intense orgasm or if I was begging her to push me harder and see what was waiting for me on the other side of orgasm number two.

She chose for me and picked up her pace, pounding her fingers into my holes and lapping at my pussy eagerly. I felt the tension build and build, pushing beyond anything I'd ever felt, and suddenly, I exploded again. Warm liquid squirted out of me and ran down my legs. Samara drank every drop, and I had to grip her shoulders to avoid collapsing to the tub floor. Once the tremors in my body stilled, she gently removed her fingers, and the emptiness was unbearable.

When she stood, and I met her eyes again, I noticed the glistening liquid on her lips and face. I groaned in embarrassment, covering my eyes with my hands.

"I'd never done that before," I whispered. Samara gripped my wrists in her hands and removed my hands from their spot, forcing my eyes to meet hers. There was a kind of prideful heat there that warmed my entire body.

"That was the most beautiful thing I've ever seen, Athena. Never feel embarrassed for chasing your pleasure with me," she commanded, her eyes still full of lust. I nodded, still feeling the creeping blush warm my skin.

After that, we washed up for real, taking extra care to ensure that any of our cuts and bruises were healed, thanks to her power. When we were finished, we wrapped ourselves up in towels, and she led me from the room.

The moment the door to the bathroom opened, I saw my other three mates standing in the hallways with hooded, lust-filled expressions. I blushed, suddenly feeling very exposed. I met each of their eyes, matching their expressions with my own. My core tightened again, obviously prepared for a round three…four, and maybe seven.

"Shoo, you three. She's still mine until she's dressed again," Samara claimed, gripping my hand and leading me down the hall to a room.

I think I heard Silas scoffing and whispering something like "no fair" under his breath, but there was a light chuckle from the others, and I felt the tense worry that had been plaguing my heart since the day we were taken crack and started to drift away. They hadn't broken us. They hadn't ruined us. We were going to be okay. Eventually.

LAZ
FOURTEEN

After Samara shooed us away after making our mate scream in overwhelming pleasure, I felt equally amused and frustrated. Silas groaned and slipped into the bathroom, muttering about needing to take the edge off himself. I closed my eyes and tried not to picture the way his strong hand would look as it ran along his hardened shaft as he thought about our perfect mate. Something had shifted between Silas and me the moment we shared Athena over the video call, something that didn't make any sense but also wasn't all that scary.

I shook my head and hurried down the stairs to busy myself in the kitchen and avoid hearing Silas' grunts as he released. I was having a hard enough time after hearing Athena's explosive climax without adding Silas to the mix. Orpheus slipped into his room, and I needed this moment of peace to feel the last few days.

So much had changed. We had a mate. Our powers changed. We survived the Hunters again.

I opened the fridge and pulled out one of the several dozen blood bags, and held it in my hands. I let my power wash over it, analyzing the blood.

O Positive. It's not my favorite, but you can't be picky at times like this.

Wait. Maybe I can.

I focused on the blood in my hands, feeling its contents as intimately as I had the acidic rain, and willed it to shift. To change. There was no bright light or tingling sound, but when I checked the contents of the blood again, feeling its chemical makeup, I gasped with shock.

AB Positive.

I'd changed it.

A gleeful chuckle escaped my lips, and I took a slow, languid sip of the shifted blood, which was delicious. Nowhere near the taste of my mate's blood, but tasty nonetheless. The strength was returning to my body by the second, and after a moment, I felt back to normal. Physically, at least. The mental damage would take more than a bag of blood to recover. I took only a few sips before returning the bag to the fridge. I had no idea how long we'd be here, and we needed to conserve as much as possible.

I heard delicate footsteps come down the stairs, and I turned to greet her with a soft smile. Samara looked exhausted, but her eyes held a sort of sweet satisfaction to it, no doubt a byproduct of her shower with our mate.

"You need to rest," I noted, indicating to the bar stool at the kitchen counter. She sat and let her head rest in her hands, releasing a soft sigh.

"I need to check on the Hunter first," she replied.

"We should probably stop calling him that," I pointed out, and Samara nodded.

"I suppose you're right. He's probably just as hated by the Hunters as we are right now," she said sadly.

"Do you want me to come down there with you?" I asked as she glanced toward the door to the basement, a look of trepidation on her face.

"He can't hurt me," she stated, and I nodded.

"I know that." I waited as she looked back at me and then nodded gently. Pushing off the counter, I moved across the floor toward the basement door and opened it, removing the several locks that Orpheus had installed.

"Let's go," I said, gesturing for her to lead the way down the stairs. The basement was precisely what I would have expected from a log cabin. The smell of must was thick as we ventured down the creaking wooden stairs. If we both tried to stand on one step at the same time, I was sure that it would buckle under the weight. The air was thick with neglect, the scent of disuse assaulting my senses with every breath.

Dust particles danced in the dim moonlight that filtered through small, dirty windows and cast eerie shadows across the worn concrete floor. The silence was stifling, broken only by the occasional drip of water from a leaky pipe somewhere in the darkness and the soft snoring from the unconscious man who lay on the sheet-covered couch. I heard his heart beating strongly in his chest, which had me sighing in relief. The way his heart had stuttered and sounded so weak when Silas first carried him out of the window was concerning. Samara did what she could to heal the internal injuries on the run, keeping him alive, but he was in bad shape. He required far more than a short burst of healing energy from a tired vampire. Hopefully, Samara has recovered enough to help him now. I'm just glad Athena couldn't tell just how bad it was. For some reason, she is fond of the Hunter... or ex-Hunter.

Samara sank to her knees at the side of the couch and looked down at the man before her. His face was swollen and covered in angry red wounds. I could barely see his left eye behind the swelling at the socket. His chest rose and fell with labored breaths.

"How is he?" I asked.

"Alive," she answered with a groan. "His father did this to him?" She asked, with an edge of anger in her tone.

She lifted her hands and carefully placed them on his bare arms. Her new ability didn't require her to touch the target anymore, but I imagine that the concentration of healing magic was stronger through touch, and she needed as much as she could get at the moment.

She quietly got to work, and I could feel the thrum of energy in the room as she sent her healing magic barrelling through Archer's body. I loved watching Samara as she worked. She was so confident in her ability, which she should be. Her healing had saved our coven more times than I can count.

I watched in fascination as the damaged skin on Archer's face slowly receded, giving way to unblemished pale skin. His breathing slowed to a standard rate, and I felt the fists at my side relax.

Sitting back on her heels, Samara sighed. "He's ok," she muttered quietly. I nodded and smiled.

"You always amaze me, Samara," I said into the basement's darkness. She smiled as she stood, touching my shoulder and squeezing once.

I looked down at the sleeping form and felt the slightest spike in my power. I shook my head, waving away the intruding feeling.

"What's wrong?" Samara asked, worry crossing her face.

"Nothing," I responded, checking in with my power silently. It wasn't angry or threatened, it wasn't trying to save me or fix anything, but it felt like it had something to show me. I ran a hand along my face and tried to pull the new power back to my body, but it was persistent and jumped toward Archer.

"What do you want?" I muttered under my breath.

"Who are you talking to?" Samara asked.

"My power is trying to latch onto Archer," I explained, feeling that distinct pull from my chest as my power slammed into Archer's bloodstream.

"Why?" Samara looked between the two of us.

My power slid into his blood, analyzing its contents and components. My power danced along the edges of his veins, and my mind was flooded with information as it studied it.

My power had never felt so sentient before, never like it had a mind of its own, but here it was, guiding me through Artcher's body.

Wait.

"What is it?" Samara asked, scanning my face.

There it was, clear as day. Exactly what my power was trying to show me. I gasped and stuttered a few steps back.

"Laz, you're scaring me," she said as she gripped my shoulders, holding me in place.

"Sorry," I said, shaking my head, feeling my power return to my control now that it had shown me what it needed to.

"Are you alright?"

I nodded.

"Yes, I'm fine. But things just got a little…complicated."

Samara watched me carefully, but I couldn't elaborate, not yet. What I'd just discovered needed to be something that Athena knew first, and I wouldn't take that away from her.

"Let's get some rest," I urged, and she agreed after a moment of hesitation.

We climbed the stairs, replaced the locks on the door, and then moved into the kitchen.

"Where is Athena?" I asked, hoping she didn't press me on what my power had discovered down there.

"She went to one of the rooms to sleep."

I nodded.

"You should go be there with her," Samara offered with a smile.

"Are you sure? She's probably overwhelmed."

She waved a hand in front of her, dismissing my concerns. "She needs her mates. And you need her."

Samara's words drew my attention to the ache in my heart. It began the moment we were taken and separated from Athena and hasn't stopped since. Not even escaping with her had calmed the pain. Samara was right. I needed my mate. I needed her in my arms. I needed to know she was safe, to feel her breathing, to hear her heart beating. I needed to be reminded that we were alive— or at least, our version of 'alive.'

She tilted her head toward the staircase with a smirk. "Go."

I offered a gentle smile back to her and then sprinted up the stairs. Walking past the door to her room, I sighed when I could hear her soft breathing. I forced my feet to head toward the bathroom. I couldn't sleep in my current state.

After the briefest of showers, I wrapped a towel around my waist and headed into the room that Athena was currently occupying. As the door slid open, the light from the hallway illuminated her sleeping form. Her red hair was splayed casually across the pillow, and her soft, creamy skin seemed to glow. My chest tightened at the sight of her, safe. Breathing. Alive. I smiled at the pile of muscles at her back, pressing her back to his front. Silas's eyes found me, and heat curled in my stomach as I moved into the room.

"I'm not leaving," Silas warned, and I smiled, letting the towel fall to the ground at my feet before sliding into the sheets on Athena's other side.

"I didn't ask you to," I whispered before sliding my arms around my sleeping mate's body. My fingertips brushed against Silas' chilled torso at her back, and I stifled a groan but didn't remove my hand. He didn't make a move to pull back, either.

"She's out cold," Silas remarked, staring down at her face with adoration and love. I pressed a kiss to her forehead and breathed in her intoxicating scent.

"Good, she needs rest," I responded quietly, letting my hand trail along her side and the oversized T-shirt she wore. I tried not to react when my hand made contact with Silas' inked skin again.

"She's the only reason we're alive right now," Silas whispered.

"I know."

Silas let his arm, which was folded around Athena's midsection, lift to encompass me as well, and I sank into the feel of his protection. His fingers trailed lines along my ribcage, and my skin erupted in goosebumps. I met his gaze, and there was a sort of longing there.

"We never talked about this," he mused.

"About what?" I asked, knowing what he was referring to but needing to hear him say it. His fingers slid along my skin again, and I groaned, pressing my torso into Athena's form.

"Whatever this is, between us," he whispered, and I think I saw a hint of embarrassment in his expression. If he could have, he may have blushed. "*Is there something between us?*"

"Do you want there to be?" I asked quietly. My voice lowered with lust.

"I think I liked telling you what to do," Silas replied, pulling his bottom lip between his teeth. My tongue darted out and wet my lips. I loved the way his eyes tracked the movement.

"I think I liked that too," I admitted in the darkness, emboldened by his touch and heated gaze.

"But-" he began, and I tried not to let disappointment flash on my face. "I think it's because of her," he continued. I raised a brow.

"What do you mean?"

He lifted his arm to run a hand through his hair, and I tried not to show how I missed his touch when it was gone.

"I've thought about our moment on the video call a lot," he began.

I swallowed the lump in my throat. "Me too."

"I've thought about being there with both of you, being able to touch her, to touch you…to instruct you on the best way to pleasure our mate. To show you how to make her scream by making you scream first." I inhaled deeply at the image he was painting. "And I love it." He smiled softly. "But then I think about having that kind of moment with you alone, without Athena, and I just-" He stopped, frustrated at the lack of words. I paused momentarily and allowed myself to think of the same scenario. Silas and I alone. It was a pleasant enough thought, but he was right. The heat was different than when I picture the three of us together.

"I think I understand," I replied softly, feeling resolute. "And I agree."

Silas sighed, relief flooding his features. I smiled and let my hand grasp his arm gently.

"You and I are like gasoline and tinder. She's the match," I whispered. "We're only complete when she's there."

He looked so relieved I almost laughed.

"I was worried you wouldn't understand," he admitted in a rare moment of vulnerability. I smiled at my friend.

"So, you want to share?" I asked, and even saying the words made my length harden at the prospect.

His eyes darkened, and a devious smirk lifted his lips. "I would love to share." I shivered.

"Good," I whispered, licking my lips. "We should discuss what we're both ok with. You know, boundaries. Just in case," I urged because I do not doubt that I'd let Silas pump into me from behind while I feasted between Athena's open legs if that's something he'd like to do, and I needed to know how far to push him.

"You're right," he said, and suddenly, his devious smirk was replaced by a shy smile. "I never thought I'd have to have this conversation with you."

"Do you want to stop?" I asked. I'd been with men before, many, in fact. But to my knowledge, Silas had never experimented with his sexuality, and I don't think he's ever been with an AMAB non-binary person before.

"No," he replied quickly. "I just… You may need to lead the conversation." He shrugged, then let his arms wrap around Athena again.

"Ok," I began, finding the words. "So, let's start simple. We only engage in any sort of physical intimacy when Athena is present, agreed?"

"Agreed," he responded, nodding.

"So, kissing. Are you ok with kissing me?" I asked, watching his eyes dart to my lips and back up.

"Yes," he said, and I instinctively bit my lip as I watched the heat in his eyes burn brighter.

"Great." I took a deep breath. "What about hands? Can I touch you?" He groaned.

"Yes," he said quickly and eagerly. His eagerness had heat building in my core.

"You can touch me too," I replied, not recognizing the lust-filled voice that was spilling from my throat. "Mouths…" his eyes closed, and I felt his hand find my side again. "Can I put my mouth on you?"

"Gods, Laz," he whispered, almost like he was in pain. "Yes, you can put your mouth on me."

"You can, too, if that's something you'd like to do," I offered, suddenly feeling very exposed under his gaze. I waited in the dark for a few painful moments while he hesitated to answer.

"Can't promise I'd be any good, but I think I'd be interested in trying." My length twitched at that, and I groaned as my core tightened.

"Ok, so…" I paused, not knowing how Silas would respond to the next one. "Penetration," I whispered.

"Fuck," Silas said with a moan, closing his eyes.

"Giving?" I prompted.

"Hell, yes. I'd give." His eyes met mine, and a moan escaped my lips.

"Receiving?" I asked even quieter, barely making a sound. He took a deep breath and slowly smiled at me.

"I don't know about that one," he admitted shyly, and I smiled assuredly at him.

"That's ok, that's why we're having this talk," I reassured him. He nodded, pressing a kiss to Athena's hair.

"But none of this matters if she's not okay with it," he said, and I nodded profusely.

"Of course, if she's uncomfortable with this, we forget all about it," I replied.

"I'm ok with it," Athena's quiet voice startled me, and I nearly fell off the bed.

"Fuck, bookworm," Silas said, a hint of embarrassment in his voice. "How much of that did you hear?"

"Enough to know it's something you both want," she admitted, looking up at me with bright eyes and pressing her palm against my bare chest. "And…" she bit her lip, and I wanted to bend down to taste it. "I want it too." Shock flooded me. "I really want it."

Silas locked eyes with me, a mixture of shock and lust, and I felt myself harden even more as my mate pressed her body against mine. Silas pressed in behind her, trapping our perfect Athena between our bodies. She closed her eyes and let herself feel both of us.

"Tell us what you want, baby girl," Silas commanded, and I had to stifle my moan at the dominant tone he so quickly slipped into. It had its effect on more than just Athena.

"I want you to kiss Laz," she begged, and I watched as Silas lifted himself on his elbow and leaned across Athena to grip the back of my head. His eyes locked with mine, and I searched his for any sign of hesitation or regret, but all I saw was lust and pure need.

I let Silas control me, relinquishing all the power to him as he pulled my lips down to meet his. His kiss was demanding and needy. His tongue ran along the seam of my lips, and I opened to allow him in. He pressed his tongue into my mouth and explored me with his kiss. Athena was pressed in between us, and I heard her heart rate spike as we kissed above her, our hardened lengths pressing into her from both sides. I submitted to Silas' punishing kiss with a whimper that he drank up eagerly before pulling back. His eyes had a red tint as he looked at me again.

"What next, baby girl? Ask for what you want to see." Silas left his hand tangled in the shaggy and damp hair at the base of my neck, and I loved how I could simply let him control this moment and feel completely safe.

Athena opened her mouth but shut it quickly, a blush creeping onto her cheeks. Silas leaned down and captured her lips with his, and I watched as he devoured her kiss. The hand at the back of my head directed my head to their kiss in a silent command, and my lips pressed against theirs.

The three of us pressed delicious kisses against each other's mouths, and I honestly lost track of whose lips and tongue I was drinking up. I was drunk on passion. Silas pulled my head back, breaking the three-way kiss far too quickly. Both Athena and I let out pathetic sounds of disapproval at the loss.

"Don't be shy, baby girl. Tell me exactly what you want Laz to do to me," Silas whispered into her ear, and I watched as her nipples pebbled against the fabric of her t-shirt. I couldn't help myself. I closed my mouth around one of the hardened nipples through the shirt, and she arched into my mouth with a moan. "Words, baby girl, use your words," Silas demanded again.

"I want to watch Laz put their mouth on you, sir," she replied breathlessly, and I pulled back from her nipple with a tortured groan.

"Anything for you," Silas moved quickly, pushing Athena up against the headboard so she could watch. Then he crawled to the far end of the bed on his knees. His eyes were dark with desire as he beckoned me forward with a single finger.

I crawled toward him on all fours as if I were under some sort of spell, wholly lost to his command. My length pulsed with anticipation. I stopped just before Silas and turned my head to see our mate. Her eyes were hooded with lust, and her legs were pressed together, chasing some kind of relief. I couldn't wait to taste her arousal, but first, I needed something else. I turned back to Silas and looked up at him as he gripped my hair in his hands.

"Put me in your mouth, Laz," Silas said, jutting his hips toward me. I was suddenly very thankful that we both had crawled into Athena's bed naked, and there was nothing between Silas and my mouth right now. I leaned forward, letting my breath dust along his shaft and loving the way his body shook. My tongue darted out and connected with the thick head of his cock, and he threw his head back with a gasp. I ran my tongue along the underside of his shaft and relished the sounds I was drawing from his lips before repeating the process two more times.

"Stop playing with me, and suck me," Silas commanded angrily.

"Yes, sir," I smiled just before opening my mouth to take him as deep as I could.

He cursed, and I heard Athena gasp as I took Silas to the back of my throat. "Your fucking mouth, Laz." Silas praised, and I preened under it as he began pumping his dick into my throat. I hollowed my cheeks, giving him everything I could. Athena's gaze on me felt like a blazing inferno.

I let my gaze drift to my mate and nearly came on the spot as I saw her legs spread before me, her fingers circling her soaking wet core as she watched us.

"Do you like the way Laz sucks my cock, baby girl?" Silas asked, straining as he pressed into my mouth again and again.

"God, yes," she gasped, reaching up with her other hand and lifting the shirt to allow her access to her needy nipples. She pinched one between her thumb and finger as the assault on her clit continued.

"Yes, what?"

"Yes, sir," she replied breathlessly, and I found myself moaning around Silas's cock. Tasting the bead of precum on my tongue.

I lifted my hand to cup Silas' balls, and he cursed again, rutting into my mouth in one forceful thrust before pulling his hips back and sliding his dick from my mouth. I looked up at him in disappointment, but a thrill shot through me at the devious look on his face.

"Laz, make our mate orgasm with that talented tongue of yours, will you?" He said with all the guise of a question, but I knew it for what it was—another dirty demand. I crawled on my hands and knees over to where Athena was pressing her fingers into her core, and I wasted no time in pushing her hand out of the way so I could taste her for myself. The combination of Silas and Athena's arousal tasted like a beautiful rosé, a perfect combination of flavors. She pressed her core into my mouth as I explored her soft folds with my tongue. I pushed a finger into her wet heat, and she shattered. I lapped up her arousal eagerly, loving the way her orgasm vibrated her whole body.

"Come here, baby girl," Silas said as she settled from her last orgasm. He had laid beside us and gestured for her to climb up to sit on his face. I groaned as she did what he asked and landed on his eagerly awaiting tongue. I watched with rapt attention as he devoured our mate. My hand gripped the base of my length, and I ran my touch along it, chasing any sort of release.

Silas' hands came up to our mate's sides and pulled her down so that her ass was pressed up to the air, but he continued his exploration of her clit with his tongue. "Laz," he whispered against her sex.

"Yes, sir?"

He moaned like he liked it when I called him that. I did, too. "Get her ass ready for you."

Athena whimpered, and I matched the sound with my own but moved closer so that I was straddling Silas' hips. My length was dangerously close to his, and even the proximity was enough to send shivers down my spine as I leaned forward and circled my tongue around Athena's tight hole.

She jerked against my mouth, but Silas gripped her hips and held her in place against his mouth. I slowly pressed a finger past the ring of muscles and sighed when she rocked back against my touch.

"She's eager," I muttered, feeling Silas' cock twitch against my thigh and pressing a second finger into her.

"More," she gasped, and I obliged, pumping my fingers into her quicker and harder. Silas held her against his mouth, and she pressed her head into the bedding above him. I let my tongue slide around where my fingers were currently inside of her, and she cried out as I pressed a third finger inside of her—stretching her walls and preparing her to take me there.

She bucked back against my fingers with reckless abandon, and I smiled.

"She's ready," I whispered, and I watched as Silas pressed his tongue deep inside her core once more before lifting her from his mouth. I kept my fingers pressed into her as he slid her down his body and hovered her above his rock-hard length.

"Say 'blood' if you need to stop, baby girl," he reminded her before slamming her down onto his length. She cried out, and I had to stifle my cry as I felt his cock against the walls within her. She leaned forward, pressing her chest against Silas and giving me complete access. I moved with her as she rode him, chasing her satisfaction. I pumped my fingers gently to prepare her for the sensation of being possessed by both of us at once.

"Laz." With one word, Silas told me what to do, and I slid my fingers from Athena's ass, but instead of pressing against her hole with my length, I slid off the bed and came to a rest near Silas' head. He tilted his gaze toward me as Athena bounced on him.

"Get me wet for her, sir. Please." I begged, pressing my hips toward his mouth, and there was only a single moment of hesitation before his mouth dropped open, and he took my length into his throat.

Athena's eyes were locked on the action, and she slowed her hips to a more sensual pulsing as she watched Silas suck me.

I struggled to stay upright as he used his tongue to bring me to the brink, getting me drenched for what I needed to do. I was going to come soon, and I needed to come inside of my mate, so I pulled back, trying to memorize the almost lust-drunk look on Silas' face as I climbed back up onto the bed behind my mate. I pressed her chest down onto Silas so her tight hole was exposed for me, and I pressed the head of my length against it. She gasped as I jutted my hips forward slightly, just enough to slide an inch inside. Silas had stilled his hips, but I saw his fingers circling her clit.

"Relax for your mate, baby girl," Silas whispered, and she did. I pressed into her more, about halfway seated into her tight ass.

"Fuck, Laz, I can feel you," Silas exclaimed, closing his eyes and groaning as I pressed further until my hips met her cheeks and I was entirely inside of her.

She was stretched so deliciously around us both, and Silas was right. I could feel every inch of his hard length inside of her. We sat there, unmoving for a moment, breathing heavily as we each adjusted to the new sensation.

"Fuck me," Athena begged, and Silas and I locked eyes before giving our mate everything she needed.

Silas pressed up into Athena from below while I pounded into her from behind, and she cried out, curses and pleas falling from her lips as we thoroughly fucked our mate. Silas pressed his thumb against Athena's clit, making her shake and tremble as she neared her climax. Silas' eyebrows furrowed as he neared his own as well. I let one of my hands slide below where we were joined to our mate and gripped his balls tightly, offering just the right amount of pressure. He surged forward with a gasp, which sent Athena tumbling into her explosive orgasm, and Silas was close behind. The pulsating of his cock within her vibrated my length, and with another pump, I was coming undone as well.

I don't know how long we lay there, joined in a way so intimate and vulnerable yet completely safe simultaneously. I eventually slid out of her, and Silas lifted her off of himself and led her out of the room to use the restroom. When they returned, he handed me a washcloth, and I smiled as he helped me clean myself. I was thrilled to see this new side of Silas—the caretaker. Once Silas was satisfied with our care, he gripped Athena's hips and moved to lay her down in between the two of us. Hands comfortingly traced lines along skin, and I couldn't even tell where I ended and the others began. We just… were.

"I love you," Athena whispered into the darkness. "I love you both. More than I ever thought possible." My heart thumped loudly as it spurred to life as it always did in her presence.

I pressed a kiss to her cheek and then her lips and watched as Silas claimed a kiss for himself.

"I love you too, bookworm," Silas replied against her lips.

With a thumb beneath her chin, I tilted her head so she would look at me.

"Love isn't a strong enough word, but it's a good start," I said before kissing her again. I felt Silas' hand on my shoulder, offering a comforting squeeze, and

I couldn't believe my luck. There was a point in my life where I never thought a moment like this would be possible, but here I was. Unapologetically myself, with people who loved me exactly how I was.

I was still smiling as the three of us drifted off to sleep.

ATHENA

FIFTEEN

When I woke, I was sated, sore, and happy, but even as I lay there in the embrace of two of my beautiful mates, I felt a hollowness and dread threaten to shadow the joy in my heart. I tried to slip out of bed without disturbing Silas and Laz, but the moment I moved, they both shot up at the waist with teeth bared and claws at the ready. I wasn't scared but rather startled as I sat up fully and captured their bodies in my arms.

"Sorry! It's just me. You're okay. You're safe," I whispered into Silas' neck before pressing a soft kiss there and doing the same for Laz. Their rigid bodies relaxed under my touch, and I sighed

Would the memories of our trauma haunt us forever?

Silas was the first to lay back down, slinging an arm over his eyes with a groan.

"Fuck, I forgot what that felt like…" Silas said, pressing his other palm against his chest.

"What what felt like?"

"Fear," he replied. "My heart hasn't raced in.. well since.." I lean down, pressing my ear against his bare chest, and listen to the heart beneath the skin. I wouldn't classify it as 'racing' by any human standards, but it certainly seemed to come quicker than it had the last time I listened to his barely beating heart.

"I'm so sorry," I whispered against him. Laz leaned into me and pressed a kiss against my back, and the three of us simply held each other for a moment, finding comfort in our collective fear.

"I need to get up," I said, pulling my head off Silas and looking down at him. His eyes looked so tired, with sunken hollow circles beneath them. I turned to see a similar look of exhaustion on Laz's face. "You both should get more rest."

Silas shook his head, but I grabbed his chin between my fingers and kissed his gentle lips.

"Sleep, both of you." I saw the moment he succumbed to his exhaustion again and smiled softly before sliding off the bed. Laz kept their eyes on me as I reached for the door, but when I looked back for one last glance before sliding out into the hallway, I heard the soft rhythmic breathing that indicated sleep.

Once I was in the hall and the door was closed behind me, I hurried to the bathroom to freshen up. Last night, while perfect in every way I could imagine, had left me feeling sticky from the fresh sheen of sweat my mates had worked out in me.

The stream of water was colder than I would have liked, but I guess I shouldn't complain. This far out in the middle of nowhere, we're lucky to have running water at all. As I washed away the events of last night, without the comforting body of one of my mates to distract me, I couldn't stop the onslaught of terrible memories from flooding in time with the water.

As the water cascaded over me, steam enveloping the small shower stall, I closed my eyes, hoping to find solace in the sanctuary of the bathroom. But instead of the usual sense of relaxation, a flood of memories crashed over me, threatening to drown me in their intensity.

The events of the last nearly two weeks replayed in my mind like a vicious reminder on an endless loop. The sudden attack in my store, fleeing for my life from a crazed Greg, throwing him over the railing, the feeling of terror as I was drugged and helpless in Archer's arms, the agonizing hours spent in captivity - it was all too fresh, too raw.

My heart raced as I remembered the fear, the uncertainty, the desperation clawing at my chest. I could still feel the cold grip of Greg's hands, the darkness of the office where I was held against my will, the overwhelming sense of helplessness, and the strangely familiar yet utterly unknown face of the man who came to see me. There was too much happening in my head, too many memories, too much pain, too much fear.

And then, like a cruel twist of fate, those memories triggered something even darker, something buried deep within the recesses of my mind but obviously not deep enough. The face of my stepfather loomed before me, over me. His twisted smile was etched into my memory like a scar, and I knew it always would be.

I shuddered as I recalled the abuse, the torment inflicted upon me by someone who was supposed to protect me. The weight of his crimes against me pressed down on me like a suffocating blanket, gripping hold of my lungs and holding so tightly that I could not draw a complete breath.

Tears mingled with the water streaming down my face as I struggled to shove the memories away, to banish them back into the darkness where they belonged. But no matter how hard I tried, no matter how tightly I closed my eyes, the screaming memories refused to be silenced. Their echoes reverberated through my skull, bouncing viciously against my mind.

At that moment, standing alone in the shower, I felt more vulnerable than I had in years, stripped bare of not only my clothes but of the illusion of safety that I had clung to so desperately for so long. Suddenly, in the chill of the water, I felt a warmth radiate through my body. It took only a moment to pinpoint the source of the comforting warmth. My mate marks heated, and I felt the rush of love and comfort flow through them, from my mates to me. They must have felt my fear, panic, and desperation and were telling me they were there. I smiled genuinely.

Healing would take more than just time. It would take courage, strength, and the willingness to confront these demons head-on. I wasn't sure I was ready to do that alone yet, but as the warmth continued to flow through my body, I knew I didn't have to.

When I exited the bathroom feeling lighter in a few ways, I went to Samara's room to prepare an outfit for the day. She was already up, so I quickly donned some dark leggings and a loose cream-colored sweater.

As I descended the stairs toward the first floor of our safe house, I made a mental list of my questions, and there were many. When I reached the living room, my head was filled to the brim with dozens of daunting problems.

Samara was right. The problems were still here, and I couldn't put off facing them any longer.

Silas and Laz were sitting next to each other on the couch in close enough proximity that they could shift ever so slightly, and their thighs would press against each other. I loved seeing the small ways their new intimacy was manifesting. Samara stood at the kitchen counter cooking something messily, and Orpheus stood with his back to me as his eyes scanned the world beyond the front window. As I approached, they all turned to look at me. They all wore casual clothing, leggings, sweatpants, t-shirts and sweaters. Which wasn't much of a shock for most of them, but seeing Orpheus, my normally suit-clad, perfectly poised mate, in sweats was startling.

"Good morning," I said with a soft and forced smile.

"Good morning, I'm making you some breakfast," Samara offered gently, and I nodded my thanks to her. I suddenly felt the pit of my stomach growl at the prospect of a full meal.

"How did you sleep?" Orpheus asked, his eyes full of concern as he scanned my body, looking for more injuries or signs of pain.

"I slept well, thank you." I crossed the floor and plopped down on an armchair across from the couch Silas and Laz occupied.

We made generic small talk for a few minutes while Samara plated the oatmeal she had made. I ate each bite eagerly and thanked her for preparing it for me. When I was finished, I set the bowl aside and sighed.

"We have a lot to discuss," I stated. Orpheus and Samara moved into the space and sat, Orpheus on the couch next to Laz and Samara on the floor near my feet.

"Are you all ok?" I asked, watching each of them as they met my eyes. Soft smiles and gentle expressions looked back.

"We're alive and stronger, and that's all because of you," Laz replied. "You got us out of there." I shook my head.

"Archer is the one who got us out." My chest tightened at the thought of him. Was he ok? He was downstairs in the basement, right? Had he woken up yet? What was I going to say to him?

"He unlocked the cage, but you're the one who made us strong enough to walk through it," Orpheus said with heat in his eyes. Not the kind that made my core clench but the kind that made my heart swell with pride.

"What do you mean?"

"You know how we each have different abilities?" Orpheus continued.

I thought back to how Samara had healed me, and I had watched Silas shift his form to look like Archer's father back at the warehouse, a shock I hadn't entirely been able to process yet, and Orpheus was able to sense people around him as we exited the warehouse, it seemed overwhelming. But I didn't know much at all beyond that.

"I don't really understand it all that well, but yeah, I know you're all very powerful." I smiled. Pride in my mates was evident in my voice.

"Well, you're right. We were fairly powerful, to begin with, which made it easier for us to hide from Nameless for as long as we did."

I hated hearing about how my mates had been on the run for so long. Never really feeling safe, never settling in one place. It broke my heart. What kind of life was that?

Then another thought occurred to me…was that going to be my life now, too? I couldn't leave grandma, or the store, or Davia. Would they stay with me? Would we ever be safe from the Hunters?

"But you, Athena. Your mate bond, your love…" Orpheus smiled as he said that word. We hadn't said it to each other yet, not out loud, but he said it in every protective measure he took, every comforting moment. He loved me as much as I loved him, and I felt it in his actions every day. He didn't need to say the words for them to be true. "You made us better."

I felt my eyes sting as tears threatened to fall at that admission.

"You gave us some serious upgrades, bookworm," Silas interjected with a laugh. "I haven't even told you all yet," he said, looking around the others and then back to me. "So, you know I can change my form. You saw that."

I nodded.

"Scared me to death, but I didn't have time to panic," I joked, remembering how his hand in mine had suddenly changed, and then looking up to see that haunting face in place of Silas'. "If I had the time to really think about it, I probably would have frozen solid."

"Well, I've never been able to change anyone else's form before," he started, and I heard the others gasp.

"You're serious?" Orpheus exclaimed, and Silas nodded.

"Freaked me the hell out, but yeah, saved our asses."

"What are you talking about?" I asked.

"I changed your form too, bookworm. I hid you from those guards."

It made perfect sense. They had seen me but seemed confused as to who I was. I was so shocked to see Silas looking like the Hunter that I didn't even bother to look at myself. I wondered what I looked like.

"That's a very powerful upgrade," Laz said with a low whistle.

"So, you think bonding with me made your power different?" I asked, running a hand through my damp hair.

"I know it did."

"I could heal without touch," Samara interjected. "That's how I was able to heal you. And I could heal them too." She looked over at her Coven with a sad smile. "Last time, I couldn't reach them. I had to sit there listening to them scream in pain as they endured the abuse Nameless inflicted, knowing that I could help ease their suffering if only I could touch them. That was worse than any physical torture they put me through." My heart constricted.

"I'm so sorry, Samara," I whispered, and she placed a hand on my knee and squeezed gently.

"You helped me save them. You made it so I could protect my family. Thank you," her eyes were shining with unshed tears, and I leaned down to kiss her on the top of her head.

"Do you know anything about what I do?" Laz asked, drawing my attention to them.

"Not really," I admitted.

"I can sense the chemical makeup of different types of liquid. So, your drink that night at the bar…" Their eyes darkened with anger, and someone else in the room growled deeply at the memory of the night we had met.

"You could tell it was drugged," I finished with a sigh.

"Yes, I could." they shook their head, obviously trying to get a hold of their emotions before continuing. "It has come in handy a few times, especially when drinking blood. Knowing if the blood was toxic or had a substance that would hurt us was useful." They folded their hands in their lap and leaned forward, their soft hazel eyes reaching mine. "But now, because of you, I can change it."

They must have seen my confusion because they pushed off the couch and rushed to the kitchen immediately. They returned with a glass of water and put it in my hand.

"Take a drink."

I did, and I loved the way the cool liquid soothed my parched throat. I needed about a gallon and a half, but I didn't want to ruin Laz's demonstration, so I pulled back and held the glass out for them. They placed a hand around mine, gently holding both me and the glass, and closed their eyes. I watched their soft features soften as they focused. I watched the water, but nothing was happening. A few moments passed, and they stepped back, dropping their hand. I looked from the unchanged water back to them.

"Take another drink." They gestured to the glass, and I shrugged and took a sip.

The moment the liquid hit my tongue, my eyes widened. It was an explosion of flavor—strawberry and watermelon flavors washed over my tongue, and I moaned at the taste. Pulling the cup back, I smiled brightly at my mate.

"That was amazing!" I beamed brightly at them. They smiled and sank to their knees before me, reaching for my hands.

"They tried to torture us with holy water. They had it rain from the ceiling, cover every inch of our skin, and it burned horribly," Laz started, and a gasp escaped my throat. "Something shifted in me, and I knew I could change it into plain water to stave off the worst of it."

"For some of us," Silas quipped jokingly. It was then that I realized that my mates had suffered even more than I knew in those dungeons.

"I knew it was bad…but" I started, tears streaming down my cheeks. Laz placed a hand on my cheek and tilted my head to make eye contact with me.

"You made it better," they promised, and I believed them because they made it better for me, too.

"I can feel the emotions of people around me," Orpheus said quietly from his place on the couch, drawing my eyes to him. He stood then, crossing the floor toward the window and looking outside again, avoiding eye contact.

"Ever since I was changed, it's been a constant. No matter who I'm with, where I go, I can feel each person's happiness, lust, guilt, sadness… pain," he whispered the last word, and I clenched my fists in my lap, resisting the urge to rush forward and hold him. "I grew to have a better handle on it, but I could never control it— not really. I just got better at ignoring it. Trying not to pay attention when all the emotions assaulted my senses," he titled his head toward the others, who nodded with a knowing look on their faces. "But it was always there, a direct line from someone's deepest emotions to me."

He took a deep breath, and I mirrored the action. "Some feelings were stronger than others, of course, but when I met you-" he offered a sad smile without looking my way. "I felt you stronger than anyone I've ever known."

"At the diner, you knew I was spiraling," I whispered.

He nodded. "I felt your guilt and knew you didn't deserve it. Not an ounce of it."

I sighed, the fists in my lap relaxing slightly.

"Then I felt your panic," he started, in a voice so low, I had to strain to hear him. "You had that attack at the Lighthouse, and I felt it as if it were my own, from all the way across town." His face was a mixture of amused and pained. "It's never been that strong before. Never in my life, and as you know, it's been a long one." He ran a hand through his hair, messing up the perfectly coiffed image he usually sported. The man before me now was as vulnerable as I was, and a part of me loved that we were in that together.

"When we mated, I felt the power shifting, changing. It got stronger. Like a floodgate had opened, I couldn't shut it down no matter what I tried. I was feeling everyone as strongly as I felt you."

Hot tears streamed down my face again. Mating me had made his power more potent but for the worse. I'd hurt him. I'd made his life harder. I felt so guilty, and then immediately felt even worse knowing he was feeling my guilt at that moment. I felt like shit for forcing him to do all that extra emotional labor. I wouldn't be shocked if he regretted being mated to me.

"I hate that I made things harder for you," I whispered in response. "I never wanted to hurt you."

He turned to face me at that moment, and I could see that his eyes were glistening with tears. However, his face was not twisted in pain or anger. Instead, all I saw in his expression was love.

"Athena, you told me to drown it out when I felt like I was exploding from the inside out. When there was too much feeling, too much pain, too much anger, too much fear. You told me to drown it out."

I nodded, remembering the moment when he had collapsed on the stairs. I recognized the signs of his spiral. I've had my fair share of attacks. I didn't know how literal it was, though.

"You told me to tune it all out, that I was stronger than them, and for the first time in my entire second existence…I was."

My heart began racing as he crossed the room to me and sank to his knees. Laz and Samara had taken a few steps back, giving us this moment. His hands held mine, and his eyes locked on mine.

"For so long, I have wandered through life burdened by the weight of others' emotions, drowning in a sea of feelings that were not my own. Every smile, every tear, every pang of sorrow or burst of joy, I felt them all as if they were my own. But then, you - my perfect, stunning little nymph- reached out to me and offered me something I didn't even know I was allowed to hope for. You granted me the ability to turn it off, to create a sanctuary within myself where I could finally be alone with my own emotions. With your love, you quieted the noise and gave me the space to breathe freely for the first time in far, far too long."

His perfect face blurred behind my tear-filled eyes, and I launched myself forward, throwing my arms around his neck and pulling him in for a kiss. There were no more words to be said.

He drank my kiss as if he were a starved man and I was his only hope at salvation, and I eagerly gave him all of me. When I pulled back, all my mates were smiling at me, and I felt like the luckiest girl in the world despite our current situation.

"I need to call my grandma," I said, watching as their faces fell.

"No," Orpheus replied quickly. I sat back in my chair, pulled my hands from his, and shook my head.

"Yes, this isn't negotiable. I am all she has left, and she's probably terrified. I have to tell her I'm ok." I stood my ground, hoping that my voice seemed as even as I was willing it to be.

"Athena, the Hunters know where you live, where you work… who knows what Archer told them about your grandma before he helped us escape," Orpheus argued, but I put a hand up to stop him.

"That is even more reason why I need to call her."

"Athena, baby, it's too dangerous," Samara chimed in.

"What if they go looking for me and find her instead? What if they find Davia? What if they kill them or take them to get to me?" My heart rate spiked. "I need to warn them."

"You can't tell them anything," Orpheus said through clenched teeth.

"I won't tell them everything, but they deserve to know I'm alive and that they might be in danger."

"If anyone tracks the call…"

"My grandma can barely work her cellphone, let alone track a call." I wasn't going to take no for an answer.

"Athena…"

"No, Orpheus. Listen, I know I can't go back right now." I tried not to think of the possibility that I may never be able to return. That wasn't a reality I was willing to accept. Not yet, anyway. "But I *can* talk to her, and I have to. Please don't fight me on this."

I saw the expression on his face twist with the desire to deny me, but I could see the part of him that understood where I was coming from winning him over.

"Fine, but you cannot say a word about where we are. Time of day, weather, the types of trees outside the window, nothing. Do you understand?"

I nodded, suddenly feeling the weight of what I had to do next settle on me.

He offered me a tight nod before crossing to the security system on the wall and pulling a receiver from the mess of tangled cords.

My fingers danced along the numbers and dialed the only phone number that had mattered to me for so long. Grandma had been my only family for far too long. I had Davia, but she wasn't my blood. Not the way my Grandma was.

I sensed my mates quietly observing me but didn't resent the intrusion. Given the tension of the situation, I understood their apprehension. I was deeply grateful that they recognized why I had to make the call despite our fear.

The phone rang once. Twice. Three times. I took shallow lung fulls of breath into my lungs as each ring added a pound of anxious weight to my chest.

"Hello?"

Her voice was like a balm on a vicious burn. Tears immediately sprung to my eyes.

"Grandma," I whispered.

"Athena?!" Shock filled her voice. "Athena, baby, is that you?"

"It's me," I responded, sniffling.

"Oh, thank the lord, I have been going out of my mind with worry. Are you ok? Where are you?" She rushed out in one breath.

"I'm ok, Grandma. I promise. I'm so sorry that I scared you," I apologized.

"Where have you been? Do you know how long you've been gone? The shop was a mess, and we weren't sure if that man… oh heavens. You're alive. Thank God. What happened?" She continued in a flurry of questions.

I took a deep breath as her questions kept rolling from her tongue.

"I can't tell you that right now. I'm so sorry."

She went quiet for a moment.

"I can't accept that answer," she retorted, the Landry sass seeped through her voice.

"I know it's not fair, but it's what I can give you right now. Just know that

I'm ok, I'm alive, and I'm safe…right now." I don't know why I added those last words, but I already felt guilty about lying to her. I didn't want to lie to her about this, too.

"It's those people you met, isn't it? You got way too in over your head with them, and now you're in trouble," she tried to reason, and I shook my head.

"No, no, it's not their fault."

"I should have told you everything," she whispered to herself.

"What do you mean?" I asked, brow furrowing.

"Who is she talking to?" I heard the voice call from behind me. I turned quickly to see Archer standing at the top of the basement stairs. His hair was messy and unkempt, and the circles under his eyes revealed just how little quality sleep he got the night before. But he was standing upright, and that was a positive thing. Maybe. I guess… God, I really needed to sort through my emotions regarding Archer and soon.

"Her grandmother," Orpheus replied, his eyes locked on him, watching him like he didn't trust him. Which was a completely logical reaction, honestly, considering he was the one who kidnapped them in the first place.

"What?" Archer's eyes went wide, and he took a rushing step toward me, but all four of my mates were up, creating a barrier before I could even finish my blink. "Hang up the phone," he commanded with worry in his eyes.

"… I should have kept a closer eye on you, there is just so much going on in this town and with that attack at the shop. I am just so…" My grandma continued on the line. Her anxious pattering filled my ears, and I studied Archer's strange reaction.

"Please, Athena, hang up," Archer begged.

I squinted my eyes at him in confusion, a look that was mirrored on my mate's faces as well.

"Why?" I asked.

"Because there's so much that we still haven't talked about…" my Grandma responded, thinking I was speaking to her, and I tried to focus on both her confusing answer and Archer's pleading request.

Archer gave up trying to move past my mates and locked eyes with me through the window of their blocking bodies. "She knows my father," he uttered quietly. And I think the whole world froze.

"What do you mean?" Samara asked the question I couldn't.

"Why would her grandma know him?" Silas chimed in, taking an intimidating step toward Archer, who, to his credit, didn't cower but just kept his eyes on me.

"Ask her about Jacob Bennett," he urged me, and I let my mind focus on her voice on the phone. Growls erupted from my mates' chests at the name, and all I could see was the desperation on Archer's face. A sinking feeling grew in the pit of my stomach. Jacob. I knew that name, but it couldn't be…

"Grandma," I interjected, slowing her stream of consciousness. "How do you know Jacob Bennett?"

Silence.

My heart sank. How on earth could my Grandma - my sweet, book-loving, disco-centric Grandmother - know the leader of an underground militia of Vampire Hunters? How the hell would those lines ever cross? Unless…

"Athena…" she began, and her tone told me that I wouldn't enjoy whatever was coming next.

"What are you on about, Archer?" Laz asked the Hunter quietly, but he didn't respond, keeping his eyes on mine as my grandmother sighed on the other side of the phone.

"What are you not telling me?" I asked, careful not to let the fear waiver in my voice.

"Where did you hear that name?" She said finally, breaking the silence. Her voice was even, not shocked, but somewhat reserved, like she had been waiting for me to ask this very question for some time.

"Tell me," I urged in a pained whisper as the truth crashed into me. I knew. But I needed her to say it.

She exhaled slowly on the other end, and I braced myself against the wall behind me. "Jacob Bennett is your father, Athena."

The phone slipped like a bullet from my grasp, crashing towards the ground with a thunderous echo. As it fell, the earth seemed to tremble beneath my feet, threatening to swallow me whole. I braced myself against the wall for support, feeling its cold, unyielding surface pressing back against my shaking body. Suddenly, several sets of hands reached out, grasping at my arms and hips, desperately trying to anchor me in reality. Yet, their touch felt distant, insignificant against the overwhelming whirlwind of emotions raging within me.

But despite the haze of confusion, one thing remained crystal clear—his eyes. Across the room, amidst the sea of faces, his gaze locked onto mine with an intensity that sent shivers down my spine. Those soft, hauntingly familiar green eyes were framed by a canvas of freckled pale skin. His dark hair, stained with dye, now failed to conceal the truth that lay beneath as I noticed soft red roots emerging.

In that fleeting moment, the world stood still as the pieces of a fractured puzzle fell into place with a deafening clarity. Archer – the boy with the eyes that mirrored my own, was the brother I never knew existed.

SAMARA

SIXTEEN

Her body went rigid, and we were all to her instantly. I tried to keep shock from showing on my face, but I knew I was failing miserably. The face of our tormentor plagued my vision, and only now I couldn't help but see those subtle similarities between that haunting face and the face of my mate that were unfortunate evidence of the truth behind the words the voice on the phone uttered.

Desperation clawed at my chest as I tried to focus on the present, on helping her through this. Her breathing was shallow, and her eyes darted wildly, searching for reassurance that none of us could genuinely offer. I placed a hand on her shoulder, hoping to anchor her, to pull her back from the edge of panic.

"Stay with us," I murmured, my voice cracking slightly despite my best efforts to stay calm. I pushed warmth through our bond, hoping she felt it. The others closed in, forming a protective circle around her.

Once a source of strength, the bond between us now felt fraught with uncertainty. There was only a brief flash of fear and anger as I tried to separate the man who killed my wife from the woman who stood before me. I wasn't sure how to navigate this new reality. With caution, I suppose. Trust was more critical than ever, yet more fragile, too.

I took a deep breath, trying to steady myself. "We'll get through this," I said, more to convince myself than anyone else. "Together."

She picked up the receiver and held it to her ear with an almost vacant expression gracing her features. "I have to go, Grandma."

"Wait," the muffled voice on the other line called. "Where did you learn his full name?"

"I know his name because he had me kidnapped," she responded with an emotionless tone.

The voice started responding in an anxious tone, but Athena cut her off. "I have to go." Then she hung up. My heart ached for my mate and the pain she was feeling. Her eyes locked on Archer, and I knew she was still processing the explosive revelation, just as we all were.

Laz and Silas stood on Athena's other side and observed her as she took a steady breath.

Athena faced Archer, her posture rigid with tension. Her eyes, usually so full of determination, now held a mix of betrayal and disbelief. I watched as turmoil radiated from her in waves.

"How long?" Athena's voice was barely above a whisper, but it cut through the silence like a knife. "How long have you known, Archer?"

Archer's face was a mask of sorrow and regret. "I only found out recently, Athena. I swear."

Athena's fists clenched at her sides, her knuckles white. "And you didn't think to tell me? You didn't think I deserved to know that the man who had me kidnapped and tortured my mates was my father? That you're my br-" her voice cracked with flooding emotions, and she paused momentarily to compose herself. "Brother?"

Archer took a hesitant step forward, his hands raised placatingly, but Silas bared his teeth, warning him to keep his distance. "I was trying to protect you. Trying to get you out of there. Escape felt like the more pressing thing at the time."

"Protect me?" Athena's laugh was bitter, her eyes flashing with anger. "You think keeping something like this from me is protection? You betrayed me, Archer. How can I ever trust you?"

I felt my barely beating heart ache for Athena. I may not understand the exact pain she was suffering, but I did understand the sense of betrayal that was now tearing at her. I desperately wanted to offer comfort, but Athena had to navigate her reaction to this on her own.

"You're my sister," Archer said softly, his voice trembling. Athena winced at that. "The moment that I found out, I helped you escape. That has to count for something, right? I'm so sorry."

Athena shook her head, her expression hardening. "I don't even know who you are. For all I know, you could be just like him. You kidnapped me!" The mention of Jacob Bennett, their father, hung heavily in the air. He'd taken so much from the individuals in this room. His phantom handprint would forever be scarred onto our souls.

"I'm nothing like him," Archer insisted, his voice desperate with an edge of contempt. "I never wanted to be a part of his world. I never wanted this. I never wanted to hurt you…any of you," he added, tossing glances at the rest of us.

"But you did. And you're still his kid," Athena replied coldly. "And now, so am I."

I watched as Archer's shoulders slumped, the weight of Athena's words hitting him hard. I felt a brief pang of sympathy for him, but my love and loyalty were with Athena. I stepped forward, reassuringly touching Athena's back, a silent promise of my unwavering support.

"He crafted me into a weapon, Athena. He molded my mind, he painted the vampires as the villains, and I believed him," Archer said quietly, his eyes filled with pain. "I am so sorry. But you were right. You have been right all along. My father was framing your Wanderers. He's a monster. As far as I'm concerned, he's the only monster I've ever met." He said those words to us, not Athena, and I hadn't realized how a part of me desperately yearned for that distinction. "I will never forgive myself for believing the lies he crafted, and I just hope you'll forgive me one day. I'll be here when you're ready."

Athena didn't respond. Instead, she turned and walked away up the stairs, her steps steady but heavy with the burden of these newfound truths. Archer watched her retreat with glistening eyes and a furrowed brow.

"Sit," Orpheus ordered the little Hunter, and he nodded solemnly before sitting on the couch. Silas, Laz, and Orpheus were scattered about the room, their expressions a mix of anger, determination, and suspicion. The atmosphere was tense, with each of us eagerly ready to uncover the truth behind Nameless and their long-standing campaign against our kind.

Ever the composed leader, Orpheus leaned forward, his piercing gaze locked onto Archer. "We need answers, Archer."

He nodded.

"I'll answer any question you have if I can."

"Why has Nameless been framing us for so long? What is their endgame?" Orpheus prompted, looking down his nose at Archer.

Archer sighed, running a hand through his hair. "It's not as simple as you think. My father has always believed that vampires are a threat to humanity. He sees you as monsters that need to be eradicated. With or without cause."

"That's nothing new," Silas interjected, his voice laced with frustration.

"But why frame us? Why go to such lengths to vilify us?" Orpheus continued.

"Fear is a powerful tool," Archer explained, his voice heavy with resignation. "By framing you for crimes you didn't commit, my father can rally Nameless support. It justifies their actions and allows them to operate with impunity. They create chaos, and in the aftermath, they step in as the supposed saviors."

Laz crossed their arms with a dark expression. "And you went along with this? You let them continue this charade?"

Archer's eyes flashed with guilt. "As far as I knew, vampires were the villains my father made them out to be." He lifted his wrist and showed us the scar that decorated his skin. "But a person in captivity is bound to react to their circumstances." He admitted softly. His head hanging in shame.

"I never wanted to be a Hunter. Even after this," he indicated to his wrist again. " I hated the idea of hunting another living being. Or sort of living being." He avoided eye contact as he continued. "I didn't know the full extent of it until recently. The Nameless network is huge and well-established. My father is only one person in an army of Hunters who would do anything to erase vampires from existence."

I had been silently observing but finally spoke up. "How do we stop them, Archer?"

Archer met my gaze, his expression earnest. "There is no stopping Nameless. They're too powerful, too connected, too prepared."

"And if I won't accept that answer?" Silas said gruffly.

"There's nothing we can do. We'd have to dismantle their operation from the inside, and I just escaped with any chance of being the inside man. We'd need undeniable proof of your innocence, strategic moves…and death. A lot of death. Maybe they'll stop if you can convince some of them that you aren't the villains. But the ones who don't believe you…They won't go quietly."

Silas nodded thoughtfully. "I'd be happy to deliver them to their deaths."

I rolled my eyes. As much as I shared his bloodlust, we were no match for fully armed Hunters with their current numbers.

"We need a plan. A way to separate the ones who don't believe, weaken their numbers," Laz said quietly.

"I have some information," Archer admitted. "Names of key players, locations of safe houses, and I know the location of the device they used to frame you. But we need to act carefully. One wrong move, and they'll destroy everything, including us."

Orpheus leaned back, considering Archer's words. "We'll need allies.

People we can trust to help expose the truth and protect us when the Hunters inevitably retaliate."

"Are other Hunters who, like you, have been lied to? Do you think there are any people who could be made to see the truth?" I asked.

He shook his head. "I have no way of knowing and no idea how to get close enough now to find out."

"Give me the names and locations, Archer. I'll see if I can get some more information." Orpheus grabbed a notebook and tossed it toward him.

Archer nodded and began writing information on the page. He paused, his pen resting just above the notebook's surface, and sighed deeply before meeting our eyes again. "I know I have a lot to prove to you, but I want to help. In any way I can. I'll do anything I can to make it up to Athena."

Silas stood, his expression resolute. "Then let's get to work."

Orpheus nodded to Silas. "Time is against us, but we have the advantage of knowledge now. That's not nothing."

As the group dispersed to strategize, I couldn't help but feel a glimmer of hope. We had a long road ahead, but with Archer's inside knowledge and our combined new abilities and strengths, we finally stood a fighting chance against Nameless and the man who had orchestrated our suffering for so long.

I swore I heard Alora's gleeful chuckle in the back of my mind.

Watch your back, Bennett. The Wanderers are done being hunted.

ARCHER

SEVENTEEN

The cool night air was doing little to calm the turmoil within me as I stood on the porch of the safe house. Dark green trees circled the small clearing, acting as a barrier between Nameless and the tenuous safety we've created here. The Wanderers had only sought refuge here because of me, because of my actions. Every creak of the wooden boards beneath my feet seemed to echo the weight of my guilt. I had betrayed Athena, my own sister, and now, the people she cared about were at risk because of me. I wished I could fix it, return to the moment before Doctor Galvin branded me with the mark of the Hunter, and find the courage to step away like I had always wanted, even before I knew about my father's lies. I reached a hand to my shoulder, tracing a finger over the raised white lines of that scar that claimed me as a member of Nameless. Then my eyes caught on the bite mark on my wrist.

Two scars. Two lessons. Two different kinds of monsters. And yet, only one of these scars was given to me by someone who feared for their life. Only one was given out of desperation and fear, and the other out of a desire t

The memories of my confrontation with Athena played repeatedly in my mind. Her eyes, so similar to mine that it was embarrassing to think it took me so long to discover our connection, filled with anger and hurt, will haunt me for as long as I live. She had every right to feel betrayed. I hadn't told her the truth when I learned it, trying to protect her, or so I told myself. But deep down, I knew it was more about protecting myself, avoiding the fallout that the truth would inevitably bring.

My father's twisted legacy loomed over me. Jacob Bennett, the man who had raised me to believe in a cause I could no longer stand by, had become the symbol of everything I despised. I had spent years unknowingly perpetuating his lies, and when I finally realized the truth, the damage was already done. Now, I was trying to undo it, but it felt like trying to hold back the tide with my bare hands.

The Wanderers had welcomed me cautiously, a stranger in their midst, but I could feel their skepticism. They had every reason to doubt me, to question my motives. And Athena... I had hurt her in a way I wasn't sure I could ever make right. The bond we could have had as siblings was now fractured, perhaps beyond repair.

Lost in my thoughts, I didn't notice Orpheus approaching until he was beside me. His presence was intimidating and yet grounding, a reminder that I wasn't completely alone, even if I felt like I deserved to be.

"Guilt won't help you now," Orpheus said, his voice calm but firm.

I sighed, running a hand through my hair. "I don't know how to make this right, Orpheus. I've lied, betrayed the people I care about, and endangered everyone. How do I come back from that?"

Orpheus leaned against the porch railing, his gaze thoughtful as he looked out into the wilderness. "Guilt is a heavy burden but can also be a guide. Use it to remind yourself why you're fighting, but don't let it paralyze you. We don't have time for that."

"I can't shake the feeling that I've already done too much damage," I admitted, my voice barely above a whisper. "Athena might never forgive me."

"Maybe not," Orpheus replied honestly. "But you can't focus on what you can't change. What matters now is what you do next. We need your knowledge and your skills. You still have a chance to make a difference."

I nodded slowly, trying to let his words sink in. The guilt was still a constant ache, but Orpheus was right. I had to find a way to move forward, to use that guilt as a catalyst for change rather than a chain holding me back.

"Thanks," I said, meeting Orpheus's gaze. "I needed to hear that."

He nodded, a slight but encouraging smirk on his face. "We all make mistakes, Archer. I've made my fair share. It's how we atone for them that defines us. Now, let's get back inside. I found some information from the names you gave me. We have work to do."

As we reentered the safe house, I took a deep breath, steeling myself for the challenges ahead. As Orpheus and I stepped back across the threshold, the dimly lit interior seemed almost cozy. The others were scattered around the main room, leafing through some files, and I couldn't help but feel almost at ease around them. I struggled to reconcile that only a few days ago, I considered these people before me the biggest threat to my world and safety. It felt foolish now, not that they weren't formidable enemies because I did not doubt that each of them could remove my head from my body and drain my blood in an instant if they felt I deserved it. And the fact that they pulled me out of that warehouse after my father left me bleeding on the ground and healed me, well, that earned them my trust. And respect. I hoped I could earn the same from them in time.

We made our way to a small table in the corner where a map and several files were spread out. I sat across from Orpheus, the flickering light of the ceiling lamp casting shadows on the papers before us.

The file on my father, Jacob Bennett, and Dr. Kline Galvin lay between us.

Orpheus tapped the file thoughtfully. "We've gathered a lot of information about the Hunters you told us about. Samara has been combing through them to see if we can use anything."

I thumbed through my father's file, impressed by just how detailed it was for the short time that they had to find the information.

"His whole life is here," I whispered, flipping through the pages of his past. Even his brief relationship with Athena's mother, Francesca, was detailed along with Athena's birth certificate. Noticeably, the copy did not have my father's name on it, but I wasn't surprised there.

There were several pages about my mother, whom my father married just a few short months after Athena was born. Then, barely a year later, there was me. My mother's death certificate made me pause. I didn't know her, but I felt her absence. There were photos on the pages. My father, with his fiery red hair and bright smile, held me as a child with equally blazing hair while my mother stood by his side and beamed up at us.

It felt intrusive to look through his life as if it were a novel for my enjoyment, each piece of information felt like I was learning about someone entirely removed from the man I grew up knowing. Who was this loving father before me, and why can't I remember him?

"We never knew his first name, not before you told us, and apparently Athena never knew his last," Laz stated, watching me with honeyed eyes. "Now, we know everything there is to know about him."

I nodded, closing the file and sliding it across the table, trying to ignore the sting in my eyes.

"Yes, we've gathered a lot of valuable information so far, but this Doctor Kline Galvin remains an enigma. His records are sparse, almost as if they've been deliberately altered." Orpheus looked down at the file and scrunched his brow in frustration.

I nodded, reaching for the pages and taking a few moments to study the documents. I immediately saw what they were referring to. "It's more than just altered. It's like they've been forged. Everything here feels fabricated."

Orpheus leaned closer, his eyes narrowing as he scanned the documents. "We do know that he's exceptionally skilled at covering his tracks. It's almost as if he never existed before a certain point. No childhood records, family history, or records of ever graduating from any institution with a doctorate program in Occult Studies. Everything starts abruptly about fifteen years ago."

"My dad said that a member of the Galvin line has been leading Nameless for as long as it's been around. We're talking centuries here."

"There's nothing here about any family," Silas said from behind the computer screen.

"If his identity is a complete fabrication, then who is he really? And why go to such lengths to hide his past?" Samara interjected.

Orpheus picked up the single photograph he'd managed to find, an image of a masked Galvin, his posture rigid and composed. Those blue eyes were just as searing as I remembered. "There's got to be a reason. Maybe he's not who he claims to be, or perhaps he has a connection to the vampire community that they're trying to conceal."

I frowned, considering the implications. "If that's true, then exposing his real identity could be our key to unraveling their entire operation. But we need more evidence. Something concrete."

"I have a few contacts who might be able to help us trace forged documents, but I haven't spoken to them since before we were captured the first time. It's risky, but it might be our best shot." Laz interjected.

I glanced around the room, noticing the weary faces of our group. We were all running on fumes, but this lead could be the breakthrough we needed. "If we can find even a shred of his true identity, it could turn the tide in our favor."

Orpheus nodded, determination etched on his face. "Make the call, Laz. In the meantime, we should keep a close eye on the Hunters. They're bound to make a move soon, especially if they are as close to Athena's Grandma as you made it seem."

"Agreed," I said, feeling a renewed sense of purpose. "And Orpheus, thank you. For everything. I know it's not easy to trust me after all that's happened."

Orpheus's expression softened slightly. "Let's focus on bringing Galvin down, clearing our names, and keeping my family safe."

I didn't have the heart to say out loud that clearing their names wouldn't be enough. There were some Hunters who would kill them on mere principle. No, in order to truly save The Wanderers from Nameless, there needed to be no more Nameless.

As Orpheus stood, I returned my attention to the table and the file on Galvin. The man's cold, calculated gaze stared back at me from behind the mask of the Hunter, a silent challenge. We were on the brink of something big, and our next steps could change everything.

With a deep breath, I began organizing our notes, determined to piece together the puzzle of Doctor Kline Galvin.

ATHENA

EIGHTEEN

I sat on the edge of the worn mattress in my tiny room at the safe house, the walls closing in on me with every passing second. The truth felt like a vice around my heart, squeezing tighter with each breath I took. Archer was my brother. The man who had betrayed us, the one I had struggled to trust, was my flesh and blood. And the monster who had orchestrated our suffering, who had tortured my mates, was my father.

Jacob Bennett. The name echoed in my mind like a curse. I felt sick to my stomach, a deep sense of betrayal coursing through my veins. How could this be? How could the man responsible for so much pain be the man who brought me life?

Was I destined to have the world's worst father figures?

I hugged my knees to my chest, rocking slightly as I tried to make sense of it all. My thoughts were a chaotic jumble, each more painful than the last. I had always prided myself on my strength and ability to face any challenge head-on. I had to be strong after losing mom. It was either that or fall apart. But this... this was different. This was a betrayal that cut to the core of who I was.

The memories of our capture flashed through my mind—the fear, the helplessness, the anger. All orchestrated by the man who had given me life. I couldn't reconcile the image of a father with the cold, ruthless man I met in that office. What kind of man could do that to his own daughter? What kind of monster had I come from?

A knock on the door pulled me from my thoughts. It was Orpheus, his presence a comforting anchor in the storm of my emotions. He stepped inside, closing the door quietly behind him. His eyes were filled with concern as he moved to sit beside me on the bed, wrapping an arm around my shoulders.

"I'm here," he said softly, his voice a soothing balm to my frayed nerves.

I leaned into his chest and rested my head on his sturdy shoulder, drawing strength from his warmth. "It's too much, Orpheus. I don't know how to process any of this."

"I know," he murmured, pressing a gentle kiss to my temple.

Tears welled in my eyes, and I let them fall, the weight of the revelations finally breaking through my defenses. "How is this possible?"

He didn't answer but brushed my hair behind one of my ears.

I wiped at my eyes, frustration and sorrow mingling in my heart. "How do I come to terms with the fact that my father is the man who has done all of this?"

"I wish I had the answers for you, little nymph," Orpheus said, his tone careful.

I took a deep breath, trying to steady the turmoil inside me. The truth was excruciating, but I knew I wasn't alone. With Orpheus by my side and the others supporting us, I knew I could face whatever came next. I could survive this. My father might be a monster, but I refused to let his actions define me. We would expose him, stop him, and find a way to heal the wounds he had inflicted.

"What is our plan?" I asked.

He ran a hand idly down my spine. My skin erupted in goosebumps with each pass of his talented fingers.

"We looked into some of the names that Archer gave us or higher-ups in the organization. Information is power right now."

I nodded but felt my chest tighten.

"How are we going to take down an entire organization?" I suddenly was intimately aware of just how…human… I was. My mates were powerful vampires with abilities beyond imagination, made even stronger now by the bond we share. Hell, even the other human in our group now was a trained Hunter who managed to take all four of my mates down alone. I was just…me.

"Are you going to tell me what that face you're making is all about, or am I going to have to turn my power back on?" Orpheus teased, but there was genuine concern in his tone.

I sighed. "I was just thinking about how useless I would be in a fight against Nameless." I looked up at him, and he was gazing lovingly back at me with a soft smile.

"You're not useless, not by a long shot. You made us stronger. That may be all the advantage we need," he assured me with another kiss to my temple. I sat up, turning my torso to face him. The bed creaked under the movement.

The moon was hanging low in the sky, casting eerie shadows through the window of our tentative safety. The weight of my inadequacy felt like iron shackles. My mates, The Wanderers, were skilled and fierce, but even they couldn't always protect us. I hated feeling like a liability, someone who needed saving rather than someone who could fight alongside them.

The thought of becoming a vampire had crossed my mind before, in fleeting moments of desperation, tied in that room alone and separated from my mates. But now, it felt like the only viable option. If I were turned and became one of them, I could fight. I could be the weapon we needed against my father and his Hunters. Honestly, the idea both terrified and exhilarated me, a desperate hope mingled with fear of the unknown. I loved my Wanderers, and the idea of a forever with them was more pleasant than I expected, but then there was the thought of those I'd leave behind. Outlive.

I wrapped my arms around myself, trying to calm the storm inside. Would becoming a vampire really solve anything? Would it make me stronger, or would it simply add another layer of complexity to an already impossible situation? Could I add more stressors to our tenuous stability? The hunger, the immortality, the Hunters—all of it.

I thought about my mates. How would they react to my decision? Would they be happy, or would they try to stop me? And Laz—wise, thoughtful Laz—they had been clear about this choice. About the gravity of such a transformation. Becoming a vampire wasn't a decision to be taken lightly. It was a complete overhaul of one's existence. And for some, it may have been exactly what was needed. But I love my little life as a bookseller in Maine. As much as I tried to escape it, it has become a part of me. Would I be ready to leave it all behind?

I took a deep breath, trying to steady my thoughts. Could I really go through with it? Could I willingly choose to become what my father, my own flesh and blood, hates so deeply? Could I leave my grandma and Davia behind to grow as I remain forever unchanged? The thought of losing more people because of my own helplessness gnawed at me. I had to do something. I couldn't stand by and watch as the people I loved suffered and died.

I sighed. I needed to talk to Orpheus. He was the only one who could help me sort through the chaos in my mind. Laz would try to convince me to think it through. Silas would go through with the change before I even got the sentence out, and Samara would have concerns that kept her from following through. Orpheus, though, would look at this logically. I knew he wouldn't be happy initially, but I had to ask at least. I had to explore every option, no matter how terrifying.

"You should turn me," I whispered as quietly as possible. I wasn't sure if any of the others would be trying to listen in.

Orpheus's heart thumped heavily once.

"No."

His jaw tensed, and his eyes darkened slightly as he firmly responded.

"Orpehus-" I began.

"No," he replied again, standing from the bed. "No, Athena."

"Why not?" I begged in a rushed whisper, jumping to my feet and crossing the room toward him. He quickly brushed past me and crossed to the window.

"Why?" he scoffed as if it were the most ridiculous thing to ask.

A slight pain shot through my chest. Did he not want me to have forever with him? It was petty and childish, but I felt my eyes well with tears, and my stupid heart began to tear.

"Athena, love," he cooed in a pained whisper. When my eyes found him again, he had an expression on his face that I could only place as regret. He pressed a hand to his chest and took a deep breath. "I swear that's not it." He must have unblocked his power because he was staring at me like he could read me so clearly. "I want to spend eternity with you. I've wanted that from the moment my mark appeared on your perfect skin." My fingertips idly traced the raised lines in the shape of a cracked lightning on my throat. I felt my connection with him thrum brightly, and he stifled a moan at the feeling.

"Look where we are right now." He gestured to the window. "We are in a safe house because we are being *hunted* for what we are. Why would you ever think I'd put you through that? I couldn't live with myself if I subjected you to a life of being on the run."

I stepped closer to him, trying to draw his eyes to mine despite how hard he tried to avoid my gaze. "It doesn't matter if I'm a human or a vampire. If you're running, I am, too."

A tear slid down my cheek, and he stepped forward, closing the gap between us to wipe it away. His chest pressed against mine as I looked up into his face. He wore so many emotions in his expression, so vulnerable and open in a way that I knew was hard for him.

"I am so desperately in love with you," he said gently, and the mark on my throat burned warmly.

"So turn me," I answered, admittedly taking slight advantage of this moment of vulnerability.

He sighed, pressing his hand to my cheek.

"It's dangerous," he argued.

"Arguably, being a human right now is dangerous, too," I replied.

"Your grandma and Davia…"

"Would understand if and when I get the chance to tell them."

"Your father…"

"That man is not my father," I interjected.

"This isn't something you can take back, Athena." He brushed some hair behind my ear.

"I know that."

"I don't remember my parents," he whispered quietly, and I gleaned up at him. He made himself busy running his fingers along my hair and shoulder, looking as if he was lost in his own mind. "I assume I had some, once."

My heart tightened.

"The longer you live in this second existence, the more you lose hold of the first," he admitted in a pained whisper.

My heart raced as the realization hit me.

"I didn't notice it until about twenty years in. I'd have blank spots in my memory. Places where things used to be so clear were muddled. After fifty or so years, I couldn't place simple details anymore from my life before I was this," he gestured to himself. "After a century, the names, the places, the feelings, they were all gone. Even if I tried, I couldn't place them." He sighed. "Now? I don't even know if I had family or friends. A life? I can't recall. It's not there anymore. As if I was born the moment I became a vampire, and anything and anyone that came before is gone forever."

My mind immediately drifted to my mom. Her beautiful red hair, her atrocious singing voice, her eccentric dance moves, her love, her heart. I felt a sob break free from my lips.

"It wouldn't be immediate, but over time, she'd be gone, Athena."

Did that change things?

Yes.

No.

Losing her memory meant also losing all memory of *him*. Which arguably would be a benefit.

Dammit.

I withdrew from Orpheus and returned to the bed, climbing onto it and holding my knees to my chest.

"If you want an eternity with us, then we will turn you one day, I promise. When things are safer, and you have thought it through, we will. But, if you want to live a long and healthy human life, that's what we want, too." He settled onto the bed next to me.

"What is that? Fifty, maybe sixty years? Less if I get my mother's disease," I spat. "That's not enough time."

"Eternity isn't enough, Athena." He pressed a kiss to my lip. I tasted the salted liquid of my tears between us. "It never is. But, if I only got one day, I'd still consider myself a lucky man."

I knew we were far from done speaking about this, but his words stirred something so vulnerable in my chest. The part of me that needed his hands, his lips, his love. I leaned forward and let my lips sink into his. His hands cupped my face as he eagerly drank in my kiss. His tongue darted across my bottom lip, and I moaned breathlessly.

Swinging a leg across his lap, I straddled him, not unlike I had that first time on the boardwalk, and I pressed my core against his hardening length.

"Make love to me, Orpheus," I whispered against his lips, and he groaned.

"As you wish," he replied with a devilish smirk. In an instant, his pants were down around his ankles, and he was ripping the leggings and the cream sweater off of me, exposing me deliciously to him.

His eyes scanned my body hungrily, and I relished his attention. My nipples pebbled under the cool air and his gaze, and I felt my pussy tighten in anticipation of what he was about to give me. He lowered his head to my throat and pressed a gentle kiss against his mark. We groaned as the connection thrummed, sending a taunting vibration to my core. His length twitched eagerly, seeking my hot center. I reached between us and lined him up for me before slowly, torturously, savoringly sliding down him inch by inch.

Our breath mingled as I made the slow descent onto him. I felt his heartbeat trying to come to life enough to match mine. When I was fully seated, I remained still, letting our bodies adjust to the onslaught of pleasure. His fingers dug into my hips as he breathed deeply.

"You were perfectly crafted to be mine," he whispered, and I whimpered. Instantly, I felt the burning desire to move, to slam down onto him again, to chase the euphoria I knew he could give me, but I refrained. I was happy to remain frozen in this moment of building anticipation with a man who loves me.

"I'm in love with you too, Orpheus," I admitted in the room's darkness. I watched his face, illuminated by the early evening glow, and was rendered breathless at the smile that spread across his lips.

"Prove it," he challenged teasingly before lifting my hips and slamming me back onto his cock.

I gasped at the delicious intrusion and immediately stopped restraining myself. My hips circled and ground onto him, and his answering moans were exceptionally motivating. I braced myself on his shoulders and rode his cock as if it may be the last time. He pounded into my pussy with punishing but loving thrusts, and I threw my head back, my mouth falling open in a silent scream as he reached the deepest part of me.

His fingers trailed along my sensitive skin sending tremors wracking through my body as he made his way to my clit. Circling the bundle of nerves, he played me like I was a fucking instrument, and he was goddamn Mozart. The sounds I made rivaled the loudest orchestras.

"I need your cum to drip down my cock," he whispered against my skin, and I detonated at the next brush of his thumb. My orgasm erupted violently and quickly. He swallowed my scream with his mouth in a punishing kiss as he pounded through my release. When I returned to planet Earth, he was smiling at me. "That's my perfect girl."

"Was that enough for you, baby?" I teased sensually, and despite the smile on his lips, I saw just how feral that had made him.

"Why don't you check?" He prompted, leaning both hands on the bed behind him and lounging back with a smirk.

I returned the smile and slid off of his cock slowly. We both moaned at the sensation. His eyes tracked me as I lowered onto my knees at the foot of the bed between his legs. "Hmmm," I mused, wrapping my hand around the base of his cock, slick with my arousal. I let my hand rise and fall along his length once, twice. Again and again, slowly, loving how his breath seemed to catch with each pass of my hand. "I think I definitely did what you wanted."

He looked down at me through hooded eyes. "That you did," he agreed breathlessly.

"I wonder what we taste like together," I teased again, and he groaned, throwing an arm over his eyes as he laid back.

"If you don't take me into your mouth in the next few seconds, I'm going to embarrass myself," he promised.

I chuckled lightly before doing precisely that. My lips closed over the tip of his cock, and I sucked him into my mouth. He gasped and gently thrust into my throat. I bobbed my head, loving the power I felt as this powerful creature seemed to crumble beneath my touch.

I licked from base to tip a few times before making a satisfied sound. "We taste amazing," I promised.

"Prove it," he repeated, pulling me up his body and drawing his lips to mine. His tongue sought out mine, and they danced together, our tastes lingering.

He flipped us over until I was pinned on the bed beneath him, and he was above me.

"I need more," he begged, and I knew by the red tint in his eyes that he wasn't asking for more sex. Although by the press of his length against my stomach, I knew he wanted that, too.

"Take everything you need," I said, and he flipped me again until I was face down on the bed. He pressed my legs apart and lifted my hips so that I was kneeling in front of him. I gripped the bed sheets and moaned as he pushed his length against my entrance from this new angle and slid in. I cried out, feeling him deeper than I had before and loving the way every inch of him was claiming every inch of me. He pressed his hips forward, drilling into me over and over at a delicious pace, and I was lost to the sensation of it all. I hadn't even noticed when he gripped my shoulders and pulled me up so that we were both on our knees, with him thrusting inside of me and dusting his lips against my neck. I let one of my hands drift down to my clit, and I pressed against the bundle in tandem with his pounds as he licked my throat.

"Can .. can I?" He asked between thrusts.

"Please," I begged, and in an instant, his fangs sunk into my skin at the base of my throat. I screamed out as another orgasm instantly ripped through me. My body shook, and he had to hold me tightly around my midsection to keep me from falling face-first back to the bed.

His cock pressed into me as his fangs drained blood from my neck, and my fingers kept me feeling like I was floating above my own body.

There was something so intimate about being fed from, and I wasn't sure I'd ever get used to it. It felt like I was opening my soul and letting the other person stake a claim inside of it. My pussy was dripping with my arousal, and I never wanted this feeling to end.

His tongue replaced his fangs on my neck, closing the wound he had made, and I missed the way his bite made me feel instantly, but when he pressed his hand on my spine, directing me to lower my face to the bed again, I forgot what I was thinking about. With a hand on either hip, he began pounding his cock into my drenched cunt, and I couldn't handle the pleasure.

"Fuck," I cried out into a pillow.

He slowed only slightly, and I felt a finger press against my ass. It was tender from last night, but just as quickly as concern bloomed, pleasure replaced it as he spread some of my arousal around the puckered hole.

"I heard you take both of them last night," Orpheus said lustfully. "Did you enjoy it?"

"Yes," I said in a breathy moan. He slid his finger into my pussy, right alongside his cock, and I loved the way it stretched me. When he removed it, he let the arousal circle my ass again.

"I don't get jealous easily, not with them," he continued, adding pressure to his circles until his finger was sliding into me and stretching me. I moaned and pressed my hips back against him. "But, I couldn't stand thinking about how I've never had you here." He ensured I knew exactly where he was referring by sliding a second finger in, and I bit down on the pillow at the delicious stretch. "Can I take you here, little nymph?" He asked gently.

"Please, do it," I begged eagerly. He chuckled darkly and pulled his cock from my pussy. I felt my arousal slide down my thighs, and the moment I began to whimper at the loss of him, I felt his tip press into my ass.

"Relax for me, baby." He ordered, and I did as he asked. Several seconds passed as pain blurred with pleasure. Soon, he was fully seated in my ass, and I was desperately pressing back into him, seeking release. My fingers played with my clit as he began to move.

"You take my cock so perfectly," he praised just as he began to press forward quicker and with more force. Between the pressure of his perfect cock in my ass and my fingers rubbing my clit, I fell apart again. This time, I heard Orpheus follow me with a curse.

Moments later, Orpheus and I had cleaned up and climbed naked into the bed. I laid a head on his chest and hooked a leg over his as we lay together in the blissful afterglow.

"That was beautiful," I whispered into the room's darkness.

He trailed his fingers along my spine.

"Every moment with you is beautiful."

"We could have forever," I whispered. He sighed.

"I know, but I want a forever with you that's not born out of fear," he answered.

"I could help fight."

"I won't change the course of your life because I'm afraid of a little Hunter, Athena." He said it in such a definite tone that I knew he wasn't willing to budge right now. Honestly, I wasn't sure I wanted him to yet. The thought of losing all memory of the woman who raised me was too painful to bear right now.

"Ok, we will put a pin in it... For now," I relented, and I heard him sigh with relief. I buried my head into his shoulder and tightened my hold around his muscular body. God, this man's body should be studied—the perfect ridges of abs, the "v" shape that graced his lower abdomen. Just looking at him had my body wriggling with eager neediness.

I felt so sated, yet a part of me burned for more. I felt like I always would always want more when it came to my mates. Orpheus was right. Eternity would never be enough for us.

"Well, well, well," Orpheus teased. "You still need more?" I felt my face flush with embarrassment.

"Turn that emotion radio off," I said playfully, slapping a hand gently on his chest. He laughed.

A gentle knock on the door sounded, and I didn't bother covering up my naked body because 1. Pretty much everybody in this house had seen me naked already, and 2. If it was one of my other mates, I wanted them to have easy access to offer me the second round I was somehow still in the mood for.

"If that's you, Archer, go away," I called out, a twinge of anger gripping my heart at the thought of the man who was apparently my brother.

"It's me," Samara's voice filtered through the door.

I felt my pussy clench at the thought of her tasting just how aroused I was.

Orpheus laughed again, and I slapped him once more.

"Come in, Samara," Orpheus said, pulling the blanket over to cover himself and leaving me exposed.

She slid through the door, shutting it behind her, and smiled at the sight before her. "Thank you for covering yourself, Orpheus. I would have hated to have to bleach my eyeballs today."

He chuckled, shaking me.

"You're welcome," he said. "What's up?" He asked.

"Well, Archer was asking if he could talk to Athena," she said sheepishly, looking over at me. I felt my fists clench at my side.

"I don't want to talk to him," I replied quickly.

"That's what I told him, but he insisted I ask." She shrugged, and I suddenly felt the flood of love overtake the anger. My mates were always protecting me. I wish they had been there for me all those years ago.

"Athena," Orpheus whispered gently, and I instantly knew what he was going to say.

"I can't," I said.

"Maybe just hear him out?" He prompted, and I scoffed. "Ok, I could kill him for you if you'd rather that?" He offered, and a genuine laugh escaped my lips. He smiled brightly at me.

"That might be a little drastic, but I appreciate having the option."

I looked over at Samara and saw that her eyes were tailing my naked body hungrily, and instantly, all thoughts of anything else were long gone.

"Samara," Orpheus whispered. "I think our mate needs you to taste her." My stomach tightened at the thought of her tongue sliding through my folds, and her eyes glistened with a look that told me she was picturing the same.

"Does she?" She asked, moving toward the bed.

Orpheus manipulated my body around until I was settled between his legs, my back against his chest, and my legs spread wide for my other mate. I gasped at the fast movement, and both my mates chuckled at my shock.

Samara stalked forward like a predator about to feast on her prey, and I couldn't wait for her to devour me. Her tongue darted out to wet her bottom lip, and I felt my legs shake with anticipation. She lowered her face toward my exposed center, and I felt her cool breath on my glistening folds. The chill sent a shock through my body. She pressed a kiss to my right inner thigh, then my left. Slowly. Deliberately. Carefully. Orpheus' fingertips found my nipples and slowly pinched, adding just the right amount of pressure to drive me wild.

I moaned her name, and I felt her hands grip under my thighs and pull my legs even wider for her before she bent down to take the first taste of my pussy. I arched into her mouth and back onto Orpehus' chest at the sensation. She was taking her time, savoring my arousal as she slid her tongue through the folds once more at a torturously slow pace. She hummed happily, vibrating her tongue against my clit, and I gripped her hair in my hands and pressed her face against my center.

She answered my needy plea with another languid draw of her tongue through my pussy. "You are my favorite taste, Athena," she said against my core. After another glacial swipe of her tongue, I groaned.

"Please, Samara."

"What do you need me to do?" She asked, feigning innocence.

"I need you to devour me," I answered with a moan.

"Well, why didn't you say that?" I was about to answer when her fingers slammed into my cunt, and I cried out. Her tongue began assaulting my clit like it was the most delicious thing she had ever had in her mouth. I ground onto her face as she did exactly as I asked. Orpheus worked my nipples in tandem with

Samara's now feral laps at my core. Her fingers worked me expertly as she drank my arousal by alternating, licking, and sucking my clit into her perfect mouth.

"Is that what you needed, little nymph?" Orpheus whispered into my ear breathlessly.

"Yes!" I cried out as Samara's tongue replaced her fingers, digging into me. So deep I could almost cry at the euphoria.

I rocked against her mouth like a wild animal, ferociously searching for my release, and she gave me everything I needed. Suddenly, my core tightened, and the orgasm ripped through me, claiming every inch of my body in a blinding inferno of passion.

When my heart rate returned to normal, I saw Samara sitting between my legs, watching me with a beautiful but sinful smile.

"I can't get enough of any of you," I said with a chuckle. "I was so afraid I'd never see you again. Now, I don't want to ever let you go."

Samara grabbed my hand and squeezed. "I know what you mean. If it were up to me, we'd never leave this bedroom."

"Do we have to leave?" I teased.

Orpheus chimed in from behind me. "Eventually, yes."

"But not yet?" I asked hopefully and with an edge of excitement.

"What did you have in mind?" Samara asked, her dark eyes gleaming.

"I need you to fuck me," I answered.

Samara's eyebrows rose with the slightest bit of shock at my forwardness, but it was quickly overshadowed by the heat in her gaze. She shifted on the bed only enough to slip the sundress from her perfect body. Her dark skin was glowing in the moonlight, and I could see the evidence of arousal in between her thighs.

"Touch me, and I rip your hand off," she directed at Orpheus, who held his hands up in mock surrender.

"I'm just here for the show," he replied with a laugh.

Samara maneuvered our bodies so that we were both lying on the bed, my head near the headboard, resting on Orpheus' chest, and her head near the foot of the bed. Our legs were intertwined, and her core was primed to press against mine. When she pressed her pussy against mine, I moaned loudly. My clit was so tender from all the attention it had been getting, but the greedy little fucker jerked to life the moment Samara's arousal slid against mine.

We rode each other like that, slow and sensual, for a few long minutes, just relishing in the feel of our bodies against each other's. Our soft breaths and the sound of our cores meeting were the only sounds in the small room. I felt Orpheus' hardened length behind my back, but he didn't move to interrupt this moment with Samara and me.

There was something so romantic and gentle about the way Samara circled her hips to bring me the most delicious pleasure. I closed my eyes and let myself get lost in the overwhelming feeling of her. Another climax snuck up on me, and I cried out. I heard Orpheus groan behind me as I came down from the mountain of pleasure that Samara sent me to. Her breathing ramped up as she neared her own orgasm, and I dug my fingers into her thigh as she rocked her hips against mine at a punishing pace.

My core tightened as I watched my mate come undone. Her lips fell open on a breathy scream, and I marveled at just how beautiful she was when she let herself go. A few moments later, our breathing returned to normal as we lay there, a mess of limbs and sated bodies.

"That's it. I'm never leaving this room," I joked, and the other two joined me in a fit of laughter.

"Except to go talk to your brother," Orpheus said eventually, and my laughter fizzled out.

"Don't call him that," I whispered.

"But he is," Samara pointed out unhelpfully as she slid her dress back over her body. "He is your brother."

"Why are you two suddenly all Team Archer? He kidnapped you!" I asked, knowing the irony that I was firmly on Team Archer myself before the revelation.

"He also saved you, protected us, and risked his life so we could escape. That sort of loyalty makes up for a lot," Orpheus added.

I scoffed, sliding off the bed and tossing on a pair of leggings and an oversized Led Zepplin t-shirt from the pile of mismatched clothing I had gathered earlier.

"We're not trying to force you to do anything you're not ready to do," Orpheus said, coming up behind me.

"Jesus put some shorts on at least," Samara exclaimed, accompanied by a gagging sound.

Orpheus pulled his pants back on but kept his eyes trained on me. "I just don't want you to miss out on having more family."

That hit me. Brutal, searing pain caught my heart, and I felt a tear slide down my face. The darkened void that the death of my mother left behind felt even deeper, even more raw, and I could almost feel the empty cavern of pain beckoning for the chance to embrace this new family member. Cruel, backstabbing grief danced in my chest. Suddenly, the resistance melted away, and realization settled. I needed to speak to Archer. He's my family.

"That was a smart tactic," I teased through the tears. Orpheus gripped my chin and turned my tear-filled eyes to meet his.

"It wasn't a tactic." He smirked.

"Fine, well, get out of my way so I can go talk to my long-lost brother," I said with an edge of sarcasm and brushed past my shirtless mate, who chuckled under his breath. Samara gripped my hand and squeezed once tightly before nodding with encouragement.

Exiting the room was easy, going down the stairs was easy, smiling at Laz and Silas when I saw them in the living room hunched over files was easy, but seeing Archer's silhouette through the front door and trying to convince my feet to go to him was impossible. Soft music filtered through the door from the porch and I saw a guitar laying across Archer's lap as he idly strummed.

The melody was gentle, timid, and forlorn. The perfect soundtrack for the moment, honestly. He was talented, that much was obvious. I recalled a conversation we had only a few short weeks ago about our shared love for music and the way a simple song had the ability to tell the most complex stories. He said he played guitar, and I told him I wanted to hear him play one day.

I didn't think it would be like this.

"You don't have to go out there," Silas said from his spot at the kitchen island. I turned my head to him and offered a soft smile.

"I know. I want to," I said, unable to move my feet forward.

"He's helped us a lot," Laz spoke gently, holding up some of the files. "We might actually stand a chance against Nameless because of him." They shrugged as if to say they were just as surprised as I was.

"You all forgave him pretty quickly," I teased, but the humor didn't quite land through my melancholic state.

"Don't get me wrong, I'm ready to rip the fuckers arms off his body if he makes one wrong move," Silas interjected. "But I guess it's easier to forgive people after they save the love of my life."

I offered him a genuine smile, nodded to myself, and took a deep breath before putting one foot in front of the other and heading outside to meet my brother.

ARCHER

NINETEEN

I heard her footsteps before I saw her and knew it was her because of the timidness with which she approached. My heart rate ramped up, and my palms instantly dampened with nerves. However, I didn't slow my strumming as the music poured from the guitar. Music had always been a calming experience for me, creating it, listening to it, feeling it. I needed some of that calm now. Athena settled into the chair next to me on the porch of the safe house. The warm golden glow of the retreating evening sun cast long shadows across the weathered boards, and my fingers danced across the strings. I glanced at her and studied her face as she looked into the distance. How could I not have noticed the similarities earlier? We were not carbon copies of each other by any means, but the strong nose and bright green eyes were identical to my own. I should have noticed it. I should have known she was a part of my family when I met her in her bookstore. I felt so ashamed that I hadn't.

We sat in silence for a few moments as the song continued. The melody was not one I knew but rather just the product of letting my soul lead the way. Eventually, I let the song trail off, the last note hanging in the still evening air.

"You're very good at that," she offered quietly.

"Thank you." I set the guitar up against the side of the house. "I found this in the basement. I haven't played in… a while," I rambled. She nodded.

"You've been busy," she replied with a clipped tone.

I nodded, letting myself feel each ounce of the guilt that stabbed my heart.

"I'm so sorry, Athena," I whispered quietly. She nodded her acknowledgment but kept her eyes trained on the forest's edge. I tried and failed a few times to continue, but the words kept getting stuck in my throat. I knew I had to face this and confront the consequences of my actions, but why was it so hard? "I only found out a few minutes before I helped you escape, but I should have told you the minute I saw you."

She looked at me, her eyes softening. "I know, Archer. It's okay. I've thought about it, and I probably wouldn't have been able to focus enough to get out of there if you'd told me then. You made the right choice. It's not your fault."

Relief washed over me, but I could still see the sadness in her eyes. "Thank you for understanding. I just wish I had handled it better. Honestly, I'm not sure I handled it at all."

She nodded, then looked away toward the trees again, her gaze distant. "Can you tell me about him?"

She didn't need to say his name. I knew who she was talking about—the man who connected us. I hesitated, trying to sort through the confusing memories. Some are gentle and kind, some more painful and vivid. There were moments when he was a good dad—teaching me how to hunt, reading bedtime stories, buying me my first guitar, and offering a comforting presence during thunderstorms. But those moments could be so easily overshadowed by his horrible actions—the ruthless decisions, the relentless training, and the way he manipulated and controlled everyone around him to pursue this wicked end goal. Since the moment he confronted me in the gym back at HQ, I've struggled to reconcile the man who cared for me with the monster who caused so much pain and wanted so much death.

"He's not what I would call a good man, Athena. He can be ruthless and manipulative. He believes he's doing the right thing, but his methods are… questionable." I sighed. "He could be a great dad when he wanted to be," I said, my voice tinged with anguish. "But then he'd turn around and do something so cruel, so unforgivable. It's like he was two different people, and I never knew which one I was going to get."

Athena listened, her expression softening with empathy. "I can't imagine what that must have been like, Archer. To catch glimpses of a good father, only for him to prove you wrong. That must have been difficult."

"It was," I admitted, my voice barely above a whisper. That was a truth I wasn't sure I wanted to face. He was my father. He loved me. He wanted what was best for me. That's the truth, isn't it? But only *he* could decide what was best. Only *he* could determine how I lived my life and what I spent it doing.

She listened quietly, her face a mixture of curiosity and sorrow. "I always wanted to know who he was. I thought about him a lot. I was more than content for it to be just Mom and I, but you know there's always that question in the back of your mind. Now, I think I hate that I know."

"I'm sorry you never got to know the best version of him," I said softly.

She took a deep breath, steadying herself. "I'm sorry you had to be raised by a monster."

"It was hard," I admitted, my voice barely above a whisper. "But I think it was all worth it because I met you. You're my sister."

She looked at me, her eyes filled with a mix of pain and resolve. "We have to stop him, no matter what it takes."

"I promise," I said, my resolve firm.

She gave a slight nod, a sign of her willingness to move forward. "My mates mean everything to me. I will do anything to protect them."

"I understand that," I said, relief mixing with the lingering guilt. "I won't let you down again."

As we sat there on the porch, the evening shadows deepening around us, I felt a flicker of hope. It was a long road ahead, fraught with danger and uncertainty, but at least now, we were facing it together. "I want to get to know you," I admitted.

"I'm not that interesting," she replied sheepishly.

"I'd beg to differ," I argued. "You own a small business, and you protected yourself from that asshole, Greg." My chest tightened as the memory returned to me.

Finally, I did it.

I thought to myself as the gas from the canisters spread through the Wanderers' hideout. I waited long enough to ensure the mixture would take hold of the vampires before pulling my truck up the driveway and stepping into the now-destroyed front room. Athena's slumped form was hunched over the unconscious creatures. Shit, I forgot she wouldn't be affected by the gas as a human—stupid oversight. I couldn't risk her catching me here, seeing me, knowing what I'd done. My father wanted me to take her, but I couldn't stand the thought of exposing her to the Nameless nightmare.

She was frantically trying to wake the vampires slumped at her feet when I made my decision. I would get her to safety first, then return the vampires to my father. Maybe he'd be so proud of me, so distracted by the capture of the elusive Wanderers, that he wouldn't notice I didn't grab her, too. But she couldn't see me now; it would ruin everything. Even with this stupid faceless mask on, I couldn't risk her recognizing me. My chest tightened as my heart pounded against my ribcage in anger as the decision was made. I needed to knock her out. Just enough to get her to safety.

I could chloroform her, I thought, prepping a cloth full of the dangerous toxin. But that could keep her out for hours. I only needed her out for ten minutes. Sliding the tainted cloth safely back into my pocket to deal with later, I gripped the weapon at my side. My hand shook violently as I approached the girl I had quickly considered a friend. What a cruel twist of fate this had been. Slamming the blunt end of my stake into her temple, I closed my eyes so I couldn't see the aftermath of her crumpled body on the ground.

Instantly, I felt sick. Guilt and pain bubbled up in my chest, nearly making me lose the contents of my stomach, but I forced it down. I couldn't lose my nerve yet. I couldn't even look at her face as I scooped her off the floor and set her in my truck. Her head slumped gently against the passenger side window. One good thing about it being early in the season was that there weren't many people around when I gently lifted her from my truck and made my way to her store. She would be safe here. Safer than where I was going. I took one last look around the quaint bookstore. Despite the broken front window that was now boarded up, it was a beautiful little sanctuary. I had deeply enjoyed my time there and found myself already missing the afternoons I would spend in the front window with Athena and a cup of coffee. Once I was sure she was safe, I offered her a silent goodbye and slipped out the back door.

I hurried back to the beach house and got to work on dragging the creatures from the wreckage into the bed of my truck. I've never felt so disgusting. With each body piled in the back, I felt the sickly chill of my father's pride, but the guilt was overwhelming in a way that invaded my senses. I didn't feel like myself anymore. How could I? I was just as bad as the creatures in the bed of my truck. I was the monster. I ripped off the mask and tried to drag cool breaths into my constricted lungs as I drove away, intent on leaving this town behind and never looking back when Athena stumbled into the road in front of me. I barely stopped the truck in time to avoid hitting her.

The first look at her had the blood draining from my face. Blood coated her pale skin, and her face was swollen and red. My breath caught in my throat. She wasn't like this when I left her only moments ago. What the fuck happened?

I did this to her. I left her alone. I hurt her.

"Holy shit, Athena. What the hell happened to you?" I asked, sprinting from the car to where she stood, barely remaining upright, on the street before me. Her balance shifted, and I gripped her arms to help her stand. Tears slid down her cheeks. "Athena, talk to me. What happened?" I asked forcefully.

I was seeing red, ready to kill whoever did this to her and then punish myself because I put her in that position.

"Greg," she whispered, and I cursed under my breath. The worst-case scenarios

flooded my brain. I left her there unconscious. He could have done anything to her... what if... No. I shook my head and focused back on Athena. I needed to be present to help her. Her legs gave out beneath her, and I slid my arm around her waist and helped her toward my truck.

"Whoa, okay, okay. Here," I whispered, setting her gently against the truck's frame.

"I'm dizzy," she said, gripping the side of the bed and breathing heavily.

"I have some water in my truck. I'll get it." My heart was racing. I couldn't leave her like this. This was my fault. I needed to help her, but how was I supposed to help her with a pile of bodies in the back of my car? I reached into my cab and fumbled for a bottle of water from the bag of vampire-killing weapons I had stashed inside. I couldn't exactly take her to the hospital or the police station with my current...uh...cargo.

"Here, drink this," I said, offering her the bottle. She looked like she had seen a ghost, her eyes focused on something in the back of the truck. "What's wro-" Then I saw it. One of the creature's hands was poking out from beneath the tarp—an unfortunately very distinct hand with recognizable tattoos. I groaned in frustration. How fucking careless could I be? Then guilt flooded my veins. I couldn't imagine what thoughts were running through her mind.

"I can explain, I swear." But I knew I couldn't, and I knew she wouldn't listen. I saw it in her eyes, how her breathing staggered in fear and panic. She was looking at me like I always looked at my father, and I hated how it felt. She opened her mouth to scream, and without thinking, I slid the cloth from my pocket, praying that the toxin was potent enough to work. I clamped my hand across her open mouth and held her body up as she struggled against my hold.

Disgust, anger, fear, hatred.

I had never wanted to disappear more than in that moment.

"I'm sorry," I whispered through sobs that threatened to escape. When her violent struggle slowed and her emerald eyes shut, I helped her into the cab of the truck again, but this time, she wasn't going to her store. She wasn't going home. She couldn't now.

She saw my face. She knew who I was.

She was coming with me.

And there was nothing I could do to stop it.

"I need to apologize, Athena," I started, clearing my throat from the emotions the memory had brought back. "I hurt you."

"I know," she responded with a soft sigh.

"I didn't want to. I wanted to keep you safe, away from all of this." I jumped out of the chair and gestured to the safe house, which was only necessary because of my actions. "I tried to keep you out of it, but then…" I choked up, and tears slid down my cheek. "I swear if I had known Greg would have found you there, I never would… I swear…" I said through body-wracking sobs.

She placed a hand on my shoulder. "Greg wasn't your fault."

"But everything else was." I was broken. There was no other way to describe it. She didn't argue but watched me with glistening eyes. "I spent so long trying to stay on the outskirts of Nameless. Taking only the most meaningless jobs, the least drastic. I didn't want the life dad had planned for me. So, I fought against it for as long as I could. But-" I wiped the tears away and tried to steady my breathing. "I made a mistake, Athena. I let him drag me in and convince me it was the right path, and I feel… I feel like I lost myself along the way."

I felt my knees buckle, and I fell to them on the porch. Athena was quick to join me, kneeling beside my weeping form. She threw her arms around me and pulled me into an embrace that I didn't deserve, but I was selfish enough to accept.

"You made mistakes," she started. "Bad ones." She gripped my chin and turned my head to face her. My gaze met hers, and I saw love there, the kind I remembered seeing in my mother's eyes. "We are not defined by the mistakes we make, Archer. We are defined by what we choose to do next."

I sank into her hold. "I'm so sorry, Athena."

"I forgive you," she replied, and a weight so heavy and violent on my soul seemed to dissipate.

A sudden rustling in the tree line caught my attention. My chest tightened with fear, and I saw the same fear painted on Athena's face as we helped each other stand. "Did you hear that?" She asked, glancing out into the darkness. I nodded, instinctively reaching for my stake, which wasn't there. In an instant, the Wanderers had exited the house and joined us on the porch, their bodies poised for an attack.

"Maybe it's an animal?" Athena said hopefully, but I knew as well as she did that we would not be that lucky.

The silence lasted only a moment before the nightmare confronted us face to face.

The Hunters from Nameless had found us.

At least a dozen Hunters poured into the clearing, armed with violent weapons that I recognized. Before I could react, Silas, Orpheus, Samara, and Laz sprang into action, rushing past us into the open field. Their movements were a blur of speed and precision, honed by years of experience. Silas shouted over his shoulder, "Athena, get inside! It's not safe out here."

Athena's face twisted in frustration. "I want to help!"

"No, Athena. Please. Go inside," Orpheus commanded, his tone leaving no room for argument. Reluctantly, she retreated into the house, her eyes never leaving the chaos unfolding outside.

I turned my attention to the Hunters emerging from the trees. I recognized them immediately—familiar faces twisted with determination. I counted quickly. Fifteen figures spilled into the clearing. Conflict tore through me. Could I really defend myself against the people I grew up with? Could I hurt them if it came down to it?

My hesitation vanished as I watched an arrow pierce Laz's shoulder. They cried out in pain, the impact knocking them off balance. Instinct took over, and I rushed to their side. The arrow was tipped with garlic, its noxious scent filling the air.

"Laz, hold still," I said, my voice steady despite the chaos. I knew how dangerous the arrow was and how to remove it before the poison spread. Carefully, I grasped the shaft and pulled it out, hooking it at just the right angle. The garlic burned my fingers. Laz gritted their teeth, their fangs bared in pain, but I wasn't afraid of them in the slightest. In fact, all I felt was worry for their safety.

"Thanks, Archer," they said through clenched teeth, already healing from the wound.

I didn't have time to respond because the battle around us intensified. Silas and Orpheus fought with a ferocity that left the Hunters little room to maneuver. Samara was a whirlwind of lethal grace, taking down opponents with swift, precise strikes.

I focused on using my knowledge of Nameless's tactics to aid The Wanderers. I shouted warnings, pointing out specialty weapons before they could fall victim to their anti-vampire designs.

One of the Hunters charged at me, a glint of recognition in his eyes. I hesitated for a heartbeat, memories of training together flooding my mind. But the memory of Laz's injury steeled my resolve. I blocked his attack, using the same techniques we had drilled into each other. With a swift motion, I disarmed him, sending his weapon clattering to the ground.

"You're defending these bloodsuckers?" He spat at me with a venomous tone full of disgust.

"They're not the monsters Nameless makes them out to be!" I replied, blocking his next punch.

"Aren't they?" he yelled back, pointing in the direction of Silas, who had his vicious claws hooked into the belly of another Hunter as she cried out. If I'd stopped looking there, it could have convinced me of what my fellow Hunter was saying, but instead, I looked closer. The Hunter, who was being ravaged by Silas' claws, had a dagger buried into his side.

"They're fighting back. You are the ones who attacked us!" I screamed back at him.

"Us? You're one of them now?" His face twisted in contempt.

"Please believe me, Nameless framed them. They want us to kill them all… and they don't deserve it!" I begged him. If I could convince them to listen, there wouldn't need to be any death.

"You're a fool," he replied, swinging his fists again and landing a punch in my gut. I doubled over and saw as he reached for his discarded weapon again.

"Stop, Arthur, please," I begged, but the determination in his eyes was unmistakable. I swiftly disarmed him and buried the blade of his own dagger into his chest. His eyes widened, and he staggered back. Blood spilled from his wound.

"Nisi Nox," he choked out through the blood filling his mouth as he fell to the ground and the life drained from his eyes. I tried not to let my gaze trail across his lifeless form as sickness bubbled in my throat.

I guess in a way, I was still protecting the night from the monsters who threatened to hurt the innocent. It may have looked differently now, but for the first time, I actually found myself proud of the stance I've taken, and the people I've chosen to protect.

I am finally fighting for my safety, and the safety of those that matter to me.

Around me, the battle raged on, a blur of motion and sound. I fought alongside The Wanderers against those who had once been my comrades after failed attempts to get them to see reason.

Orpheus ripped the throat out of a boy who came to my tenth birthday party, while Silas dragged his claws across the throat of a girl I had a crush on during training. The clash of emotions was agonizing to steady myself against. "Please believe me," I begged again before another Hunter ignored my pleas and continued their assault on the Wanderers.

"Samara!" I heard Athena's voice scream out, and I turned to find the female vampire in the battle, each of her arms held behind her. Ropes doused in holy water, searing against her skin as she screamed out. The Hunter held a stake above his head, aimed for the kill.

Then Athena was rushing across the expanse.

"No, Athena, stop!" I called out after her, sprinting in her direction. The other Wanderers heard my call and turned to see the current situation. In their distraction, both Silas and Orpheus were dealt vicious blows by the few remaining Hunters. Silas fell to his knees, and Orpheus doubled over as the wooden stakes were buried deep into their skin. They were lucky that the Hunters barely missed their hearts.

How quickly the tides of this fight have turned.

I sprinted after Athena as she raced past the fallen bodies of Hunters and toward her captured mate. She's quick, too quick for me,

"Athena, don't!" Samara cried out, eyes wide with fear as she approached. The world seemed to slow as the glint of the stake flashed through the air, hurtling toward Samara. My heart pounded in my chest, the scene unfolding with a terrible clarity. In an instant, Athena threw herself in front of Samara, her body moving faster than I could process.

"No!" My screams echoed across the clearing.

The stake pierced Athena's heart with a sickening thud, her eyes widening in shock and pain. My breath caught in my throat, and my feet stilled as Athena sank to the ground, the weapon still lodged deep in her chest, her breathing shallow and labored.

I stood frozen, unable to react. My mind was racing, but my body was paralyzed by fear and grief. The other Wanderers erupted into a fury unlike I've ever seen, their rage transforming them into the monsters of nightmares. Despite their injuries, Silas, Orpheus, and Laz attacked the remaining Hunters with a vengeance, their strikes swift and deadly. The air filled with the sounds of battle—clashing weapons, cries of pain, and the unmistakable scent of blood. Samara took her vengeance out on the Hunters who held her back and the one who had driven the stake into Athena's chest by using the very rope they bound her with to strangle the air from their lungs.

Her primal scream of pain was so palpable I felt it in my very bones.

My feet were rooted to my spot. I was unable to move, breathe, or tear my eyes from the bloodied body of my sister as she struggled to drag in breath. Samara dropped to her knees beside Athena after the last assailant had fallen, her eyes slowly reverting to a more human color and filled with horror and sorrow. "Athena, stay with me. I can heal you," she pleaded, her voice breaking. "Please, don't leave us." She placed her hands on Athena's arms, and I saw a faint white glow emulating from her palms.

I forced myself to move, crossing the chasm of distance. My hands trembled as I knelt beside my sister. "Athena, I... I don't know what to do," I confessed, my voice choked with emotion. The sight of her lying there, so vulnerable and hurt, tore me apart. "Please, Athena," I whispered, my voice trembling. "Stay with us. We need you. I need you."

The other Wanderers joined us, having finally discarded the remaining Hunters.

"Heal her," Silas demanded in an almost inhuman tone. If I could draw my eyes from my sister, I'd see him in his full vampire form.

"She's so weak," Samara cried out, ripping the stake from her chest and pressing her palms onto the wound. Blood pooled beneath her hands and slid past her fingers.

"Athena, baby, you're ok, you're ok," Laz cooed, sliding to the ground by her head and lifting it into their lap.

"It's not working," Samara screamed in frustration and anger. "She's slipping away! This can't be happening, please, not again." Tears poured from her eyes as she screamed.

"Orpheus! Do something!" Silas screamed.

The normally composed vampire looked disheveled and weak, standing bare-chested, covered in blood, and sporting vicious slashes and burns across his skin as he looked down at the scene in shock.

"Orpheus!" Laz echoed, desperation lacing their tone.

"I... I don't.." Orpheus stuttered.

"She's dying!" Samara cried out again, pressing her hands even harder against Athena's skin. Suddenly, all four of them reached up to clutch their chests in pain as if something was stabbing them.

"The bond is severing," Laz cried out through mournful sobs.

"Somebody has to be able to save her," I whispered, reaching for Athena's hand and holding it in mine. Her breathing had slowed so much that I could barely see her broken chest rise and fall anymore. The thought of losing her, just as we've finally found each other, sliced into my heart and sent me spiraling into a devastating landscape of pain and panic. I'd give anything to keep her here. I'd do anything to protect her. She's my family. She's my sister. I can't lose her.

"Turn her," I demanded.

Samara looked up at Orpheus, her eyes pleading.

"She doesn't understand what it means…" he began.

"She'd still be here!" Silas argued in his animalistic voice.

"We'd be condemning her to a life of being a monster," Orpheus said, but his resolve seemed to falter.

"But at least she'd still be here," Samara cried out. "Please, she's almost gone."

I saw the turmoil in his eyes, something maybe the others couldn't recognize, but I could. He knew just how dangerous his existence was and how scary it was to be forced to become something you didn't want to be. Something you don't fully understand.

"Orpehus," I began, getting his attention. He turned his tear-filled eyes to me. "You are not a monster. None of you are. And she won't be either."

He nodded softly, releasing his breath on a shaky exhale before rushing forward and falling to his knees.

"Everyone, drink from her. Just a little. Make it quick," Orpheus ordered, his dominant persona fully restored. I slid back to allow the four of them to surround her. Laz and Silas each grabbed a wrist, and Samara and Orpheus settled their mouths on either side of her neck.

They sank their fangs into her skin and took hurried drinks of her crimson blood before pulling back. "Now," Orpheus commanded again. And I watched as the four of them sank their fangs into their own wrists to let their nearly black blood flow down their arms, and one after another, they placed their bleeding wrists at Athena's mouth, allowing the blood to drip onto her tongue. "Drink, little nymph, please." I waited to feel disgusted, for the fear of vampires to return, but I only felt desperate hope.

I wanted this to work.

I needed this to work.

Once all four of them had drank from her and pressed their wrists to her lips, they sat back, their chests heaving with ragged breathing.

"Is it working?" Silas asked, his eyes returning slightly to his more human and vulnerable shade.

Samara pressed her hands against Athena's form and closed her eyes as she focused.

"Samara," Laz urged impatiently.

"Hold on," Samara snapped. I could hear my heartbeat in my ears as the moment of silence allowed the weight of the last few minutes to crash over me. Fifteen Nameless soldiers were dead, scattered across the field around me, and now my sister might be following them to whatever afterlife there is.

We huddled around Athena's still form, the air thick with tension and desperation. The Wanderers had done everything they could. Now, we wait.

The night was eerily quiet, and the only sounds were our shallow breaths and the occasional rustling of leaves in the wind. Samara clutched Athena's hand, her eyes never leaving her face. "I can't feel a heartbeat anymore. She's dead."

A sob ripped from my throat, and I cried out—pain unlike any I'd ever experienced pooled in my chest.

"That doesn't mean it didn't work. We're all dead, too. That's how it works."

Orpheus insisted hopefully, desperately trying to convince himself of the truth behind his words.

"Come on, Athena," Samara whispered, her voice cracking. "You have to come back to us." Orpheus paced back and forth, his normally calm demeanor shattered.

"What if it doesn't work? What if we've lost her?" Laz spoke. Their voice was raw with worry, each word a dagger to our hearts.

Silas stood and stepped back, his fists clenched, his jaw tight. "She's strong. If anyone can survive this, it's Athena," he said, more to convince himself than anyone else.

I knelt beside her, my heart pounding in my chest. The bite marks on her neck and wrist, the ones we had hoped would save her, looked too small to make a difference now. "Athena," I whispered, my voice trembling. "Please."

Minutes felt like hours as we waited, uncertainty pressing down on us in thick waves. Through every flicker of the moonlight on her skin, every breeze of wind rustling her hair, we watched with bated breath, hoping for a sign of life. Or second life. My mind raced with a thousand thoughts, each more desperate than the last. Had we done enough? Had we acted too late? Would she survive? Would she be upset with us if she did?

The moon cast a cold, pale light over us, a stark contrast to the warmth we so desperately needed—the warmth that Athena so often brought to our lives. I felt like I was trapped in my private hell, fearing the worst but clinging to hope. The silence was deafening, a void filled with our collective anxiety.

Then, a shudder ran through Athena's body. We all froze, our eyes locked on her, waiting for any further movement. Another shudder, and then her eyes fluttered open to reveal bright red pupils. But despite the terrifying sight, relief was the only thing I could feel.

"Oh, thank God," Samara gasped, tears streaming down her face. "Athena, you're ok."

Athena's gaze was unfocused initially, but slowly, recognition dawned in her eyes. She looked at each of us in turn, a weak smile forming on her lips. "I... I'm here," she whispered, her voice faint but unmistakably alive.

We all exhaled. The collective breath we held released with a surge of joy and relief. Silas let out a triumphant shout. Orpheus sank to his knees in gratitude, letting his head fall back as he turned his face to the sky with a relief-filled sigh, and Laz wiped away a tear, their expression softening.

I leaned in close, my eyes wet with emotion. "You scared us," I said, my voice strained. I was worried that whatever transformation there was would take away the parts of Athena that I recognized as my sister, but other than her slightly reddened eyes, she was still just...her.

Athena nodded weakly, her eyes scanning the area. "What happened?"

"We'll explain everything soon," Orpheus pressed a kiss to her bloodied lips. "But we need to get out of here, now, before any more Hunters show up. And you need to feed."

ATHENA

TWENTY

My head was throbbing, and my chest felt like it was on fire. In fact, my whole upper body felt like it was alight with flames, all the way from my sternum, up the column of my throat, and to my eyes. I couldn't make sense of the jumbled mess of memories that led me to this moment. There was an ambush. I remembered that much. Then Silas told me to go inside, and I did despite every fiber of my being telling me not to. Watching from the window, I was forced to stand by and watch my mates and brother taking on skilled and blood-thirsty Hunters. Then I remember Samara's arms being bound, her screams of pain. I felt it through our bond. She needed me. So I ran. Then nothing. I don't recall what happened after that, but looking around, I saw each of their faces. A little battered and bruised for sure, but alive. I sighed in relief.

"What happened?" I asked.

"We'll explain everything soon," Orpheus pressed a kiss to my tender lips, bringing my attention to the strange taste there. "But we need to get out of here, now, before any more Hunters show up. And you need to feed."

"Feed?" I asked, struggling to sit up. Samara helped steady me, and I watched

"Your injuries were severe," Orpheus started, indicating the stake that was on the ground beside me. I tracked the movement, and my eyes landed on the weapon.

"You jumped in front of a Hunter's stake," Samara whispered. "You saved my life by sacrificing yours," she said adoringly but with an edge of pain.

"Oh, Samara, I'm so sorry," I started, reaching a hand to cup her face. "I hate that I put you in that position again. I didn't think. I just had to save you." Thoughts of Alora flooded my mind, and I felt instantly guilty for my part in this traumatic experience.

Samara pressed a gentle kiss to my lips.

"So you healed me?" I asked after pulling back. Samara glanced up at Orpheus again.

"Stop having silent exchanges and tell me what happened," I said a little more forcefully.

We need to tell her. Samara's voice echoed in my mind the way it had back at Nameless when we were able to create that strange mental link.

"Tell me what?" I asked. Samara's eyes widened.

You heard that? She asked through the channels of her mind again.

Yes, I heard that. I bit back through my mind.

"What's going on," Silas asked.

"She established the mental link again," Samara said.

As she said it, I closed my eyes and focused on the bond I had with my mates. Back at the Nameless headquarters, I had managed to create a link with Laz, and Samara was able to speak to them, but the signal was weak. And no matter how hard I tried, I couldn't do it again. But here, at this moment, I felt each of our bonds so viscerally, like they were tangible threads connecting me to each of them. They felt malleable in my hands. I knew I could pull on them as I needed. I focused on one of them and was pleased to see just how easily the connection formed.

I deserve to know what's going on. I said.

Orpheus' eyes widened.

I can hear you. He replied silently.

I was too confused and afraid to revel in the excitement of the mental connections being stronger and easier to control now.

Good, then tell me what happened. I begged.

"You weren't going to survive. We..." Orpheus responded aloud, his voice choked up. We almost lost you." I tried to stand, but my legs felt too weak beneath me. Samara and Archer both grabbed an arm and helped me to my feet, remaining close enough to keep me steady.

"I'm ok. I'm here," I promise, throwing my arms around his neck.

"I know, but.." he started but paused to breathe. I pulled back and took this time to pull my other mates into an embrace. Silas sank into my arms, finally releasing the tension in his body in the safety of my hug. He pressed a flurry of kisses against my throat, and I smiled at him before moving to grip Laz. They held me gently as if they were afraid I'd drift away at any moment. We shared a brief kiss, and they brushed my hair behind an ear, staring into my eyes with so much adoration I was almost swimming in it. Samara was waiting for my embrace, and she molded her arms around my body perfectly, sinking her hands into my hair and around my waist and pressing me flush against her body.

Then, I turned to face Archer. We had only just settled the distance between us, and I was so afraid that I would lose him before I ever had a chance to get to know him. I tossed my arms around his neck and pulled him close. He hugged me back desperately, just as afraid to lose this bond as I was, it seemed. Suddenly, a pungent aroma filled my nostrils, something almost sweet and sharp. Then I felt it– a sudden, intense hunger. I inhaled deeply, and the scent of his blood filled my senses, rich and intoxicating. And so very mouth-watering.

My vision shifted, a red tint creeping in around the edges. I could feel my front teeth extending, sharp, and aching with a need I had never experienced before. The sharp points bit into the skin of my bottom lip. The warmth of his body and the pulse of his blood became the only thing I could focus on.

My throat burned with a desperate thirst, and my mind clouded with a singular, overpowering desire.

Drink.

I tried to pull back, to warn him, but my body refused to obey. The primal urge was too strong, overwhelming any rational thought. Archer's voice became a distant murmur as the sound of his heartbeat pounded in my ears, each thump calling to me, tempting me.

"Athena?" he asked, concern creeping into his voice as he felt me tense. "Are you okay?"

I opened my mouth to speak, but all that came out was a low, guttural growl. Panic flared within me, fighting against the hunger, but it was a losing battle. I could think of nothing else but the need to sink my fangs into his neck, to taste the blood that was so tantalizingly close.

"No," I managed to choke out. My voice was strained and barely human. "Archer, stay back."

He pulled away slightly, his eyes widening in alarm as he saw the transformation overtaking me.

"I... I'm so thirsty," I gasped, my fangs fully extended now, my vision swimming in red. "I can't control it."

The realization of what I had become hit me with brutal clarity.

I was a vampire.

And the hunger was all-consuming.

As I fought to hold on to my last shred of humanity, the scent of Archer's blood was a relentless torment, pushing me to the brink.

I clenched my fists, digging my nails into my palms in a desperate attempt to focus on something other than hunger. "Get away from me," I pleaded, my voice a mixture of desperation and fear. "Please, Archer, go."

Arms encircled my waist and pulled me back against a hard wall of muscle. The loosely coiled serpent at the base of my throat pulsed with energy as Silas held me tight to his frame. His presence instantly calmed me, and the red tint that had colored my world slowly dissipated, but the fangs remained, and my hunger didn't wane.

"You're ok, I've got you, bookworm," Silas whispered into my ear.

"I don't want to hurt him," I replied in a broken whisper. Orpheus approached me with an almost guilty look on his face. The closer he got to me, the more the lightning-shaped mark on my neck pulsed.

"Laz, go get a blood bag from the fridge," he ordered, and my curly-haired mate gave me one last solemn look before rushing off toward the house.

I'm so sorry, Athena. I never wanted to take this choice away from you. Orpheus spoke directly into my mind.

Part of me was thrilled that I was going to be able to spend eternity by their side, but another part of me was terrified of losing the person I've always been to make room for this new version of myself. I sighed, closing my eyes and leaning my head back against Silas' chest.

"The mental link is stronger now," I whispered, trying to avoid thinking about my hunger by focusing on something else. "Is that a vampire thing?"

"Well, yes and no," Samara replied. "I think it's your gift."

I steadied my breathing, trying to force my fangs to retreat so I could focus on this new piece of information.

"My gift?" I asked.

"Your vampire ability," Orpheus chimed in. "Like how I feel emotions, or Samara can heal," he continued. "It was latent as a human. That's why you were able to establish the link a few times, but now that you're one of us, it's been unlocked. I should have guessed that was the case when I first heard about it."

"That's… interesting," I said through gritted teeth as the hunger returned to overtake my senses. I couldn't focus on anything but the burning in my throat and the scent of delicious human blood emanating from my brother.

"Here ya go, darlin'," Laz said as they returned, a bag filled with dark crimson blood in their hand. The moon phases on my upper thigh vibrated as they neared me. They held the bag out for me, and despite the burning thirst in my throat, I hesitated.

"You're going to be ok, Athena. I promise." Samara stepped forward, sending her mark on my wrist, humming with energy, and placing a hand on my arm. My tongue darted out to wet my bottom lip, tasting the sheen of my own blood that my fangs had drawn. The blood tasted good, like a decadent sweet treat, the most delicious of desserts, but the blood within Archer's veins was like sustenance. It called to me with the promise of fulfillment to quench this vicious thirst.

"Drink, Athena. You'll feel better," Orpheus urged, and Laz pressed the bag closer toward me.

Gripping the bag in one hand, I watched as my mates studied me with a mixture of anticipation and guilt. They were so afraid. Afraid for me. Or maybe afraid of me? Were they upset that this was who I was now? Were they feeling forced into an eternity with me that they didn't plan for themselves?

"Stop that," Orpheus commanded softly. I glanced at him, unsure if he felt my emotions or if I unwillingly broadcasted my thoughts to them. "Don't let your mind say those things to you. Don't let your fears make you feel unworthy of this. We love you, we want you, and we are thrilled that you are safe and *alive*." He cleared his throat. "We're just worried that you'll resent us. That you'll resent me." His eyes turned to the ground, and I felt my suddenly quiet heart ache.

I lifted the bag to my mouth, keeping my eyes trained on my mates in front of me. I let the first wash of the thick crimson liquid cross my lips, and the jolt of thirst was like electricity dancing through my blood. I lost all sense of myself and sank my teeth into the bag, allowing the blood to pour into my mouth.

It was like a blinding light had blurred my senses, warm and vibrant. The first drop of blood touched my tongue, and an explosion of sensation engulfed me. A heady mix of sweetness and iron that seemed to sing through every nerve in my body. The warmth of it spread like wildfire through my chest, igniting a primal satisfaction deep within me.

After every last drop of the delicious nectar was drained from the bag, I licked my lips to savor the final taste, moaning in delight at the feeling of fullness in my chest. I opened my eyes to see four sets of ravenous eyes watching me with lustful hunger, but as my red-tinted eyes settled on the fifth set of eyes, I felt the pointed tips of my fangs retreat, and the color returned to the world as the tint disappeared.

He looked at me like someone might look at a criminal. As if he was disgusted at what I had done and what I had become. The guilt overshadowed the euphoria of feeding. He's only just begun to see vampire-kind as more than the monsters from his nightmares, and here I am, proving those stories right.

"Archer-" I started, my voice finally returning to a tone I recognized as my own. "I am so sorry you had to see that. I swear I wouldn't hurt you," I promised, even though I had no way of knowing if that was the truth. If my mates hadn't stopped me, would I have hurt Archer? Would I have been able to keep myself from draining him? I'd like to think so, but there was so much unknown about my new existence.

"I know," he replied, his face softening. "I'm just-"

"I'm not a monster," I blurted out, a phrase meant for his ears, but it landed on my heart just as hard.

Archer's face contorted in pain as he stepped forward. His hand came to a rest on my shoulder. The proximity only amplified how good his blood smelled, but I found it significantly easier to hold on to the impulses now that I had fed. It helped that I had the presence of my mates at my back, knowing they'd step in if I needed them.

"I know that, Athena." His green eyes met mine, and I saw a light sheen of tears cresting. "God, of course, I know that. You're you. And you're alive. That's all that matters to me."

"I thought vampires weren't alive," I teased gently, an edge of insecurity in my tone. I didn't dare let my hope overshadow the very real possibility that things would never be ok between us.

"You may not be human, but you are alive," he answered firmly.

I threw my arms around him again, all thoughts of sinking my fangs into his throat, a distant memory as the rush of love I had for my brother overtook them all. He held me back, and something shifted in the dark void in my heart. The pain making way for a new connection to take root.

"We need to move. We don't know if they'll send more," Silas spoke up from behind me. Pulling back from my brother, I turned to see the others all agree in anxious eagerness.

"How do you think they found us?" Samara asked.

"My father might have tracked the call you made to your grandma if she told him about it," Archer replied, and I was suddenly reminded about that horrible mess that I needed to process soon.

"So what do we do?" I asked as we began to move through the clearing toward the safe house, averting my eyes and my senses from the dead bodies and spilled blood that littered the expanse. I felt Archer tense as we passed the corpses of his fallen colleagues, maybe even friends, and I gripped his hand tightly in mine. He shot me a thankful glance. "They've proven they will find us, no matter where we hide."

Silas threw an arm around my shoulders and hugged me to his side, pressing a delicate kiss to my head. Laz followed closely behind us, their presence a blanket of comfort as the chilling scene from the clearing threatened to topple my resolve.

Samara and Orpheus stopped on the porch of the house and turned to face us. The five of us stood in a circle, bodies bruised and bloodied. Some of us intimately changed forever. The gravity of the fight that waited for us weighed heavily on us all.

"They will find us again, you're right. But this time, we will be ready. We will never fall to Nameless again," Orpheus declared, his strength and bravery radiating almost intoxicatingly. He promised a future where we were victorious, and at that moment, I felt just confident enough to believe him. His eyes scanned our faces, meeting each of our gazes in turn. Determination burned in those eyes, a fierce strength and power that marked him as a man who would never be a victim again. I understood that determination in a way few others could. His eyes met Archer's, and I saw a look of understanding pass between them, a camaraderie that had my nearly dead heart thumping in my chest.

"Where are we going to go?" I asked in the darkness.

And then, as the moonlight bathed his face, I saw an emotion cross Orpheus' features that I hadn't seen since we were taken. A small smile played on his lips as he said, "Home, Athena. We're going home." Hope. It was hope. And in that moment, I felt it too.

We stood together, a united front against the darkness that had hunted us for so long. Archer and his father's demands for who he should become and who he should hate. The Wanderers and the Hunters that had kept them on the run for their entire second lives, and me and the demons of my past that haunted me in my most vulnerable of moments. We had faced unimaginable horrors alone for too long, but now, with hope lighting our path, I knew we could finally reclaim our lives.

Together.

ACKNOWLEDGMENTS

The Hunted, the third installment in the Nameless series, wouldn't be here without the unwavering support and encouragement of some incredible people in my life.

To my mom, thank you for always believing in me and supporting my dreams. Your constant encouragement has been my anchor. To my husband, my first reader, and my biggest fan, thank you for your invaluable feedback and unwavering support. Your enthusiasm keeps me motivated.

To everyone who has eagerly awaited this novel, your excitement and support mean the world to me. Thank you for joining me and the Wanderers back in the world of Nameless. Your love for these characters and their journey is what keeps me going.

Welcome back to the world of Nameless, and thank you for being a part of this adventure.